Praise for Bianca D'Arc's *The Ice Dragon*

5 Angels and a Recommended Read "Ok, I have to say it; no one does dragons like **Bianca D'Arc**. With the third in the *Dragon Knights* series, she continues to awe me with her characters and her fertile imagination. ...With a fantastic twist that comes out of nowhere, *The Ice Dragon* is very much a Recommended Read." ~ *Serena, Fallen Angel Reviews*

5 Stars "This is a beautifully written book of love, sex and sensuality...This is the first shape shifter book I've ventured into and it certainly won't be my last. Ms. D'Arc's story line flows smoothly from one scene to another with characters coming to life before your eyes...This book has hot sex and a very good plot. Long after you've put it down, it lingers with you." ~ *Just Erotic Romance Reviews*

5 Clovers "D'Arc manages to keep the story fresh and yet satisfyingly familiar simultaneously, with just the right balance of sweet and sexy bound by an engaging story...As usual, D'Arc also strews the ground with breadcrumbs for future stories in the *Dragon Knights* series, leaving her fans breathless in anticipation for the next story! Indeed, the reader is left with the certainty that the author is just as excited to see what delights this world has in store as the reader is!" ~ *Jennifer, CK2S Kwips and Kritiques*

5 Kisses "Once again, in The Ice Dragon,Bianca D'Arc produces a lovely story of dragon shifters and their human companions. Her world-building is very detailed and complex, with nary a thread left to unravel. The writing is fast-paced; and immediately the reader becomes deeply involved with the characters....This is a most excellent novel, to read alone, or as part of the series. I challenge any reader to pick this one up and NOT go on to complete the series, though! May there be many more episodes in the future!" ~ *Frost, Two Lips Reviews*

The Ice Dragon

Dragon Knights Book 3

Bianca D'Arc

A SAMHAIN PUBLISHING, LTD. publication.

Samhain Publishing, Ltd.
2932 Ross Clark Circle, #384
Dothan, AL 36301
www.samhainpublishing.com

Editing by Jessica Bimberg
Cover by Scott Carpenter

First Samhain Publishing, Ltd. electronic publication: September 2006
First Samhain Publishing, Ltd. print publication: December 2006

Dedication

To Jeanette, Pam, Julie, Leah, Patricia, Brenda, Cherie, and Liz.
Thanks for all your support and encouragement. And to my buddies
Stella, Serena, Megan, Jess, and all those who have encouraged me
and helped me realize this dream, especially my family.

Here there be Dragons!

Prologue

Salomar threw the useless girl in with the egg. He had no care for the girl, but the egg, now that could be profitable if he treated it right. Tall as a full-grown man and then some, the egg was near maturity, or so he'd been told. He and his men had run off the wild dragon guarding the egg. It hadn't been easy, but with the help of his pet witch, it had been done. The great wild Ice Dragon took to the skies, blinded and without memory of the egg she left behind, thanks to the enchantments of the North Witch, Loralie.

Salomar fancied himself king of the Northlands. He had an army, a pet witch, and many slaves to do his bidding. That the Northlands were little more than frozen crags of rock in between mountainous glaciers didn't bother him. He was king of it all. Or so he thought.

The slave girl was older than she appeared. Half-starved from years of deprivation, still she managed to cling to life and the illusion of youth she cultivated. It protected her somewhat from the brigands Salomar called his *knights*. The word was wasted on the ruffians muffled in furs and stinking to the heavens. The men rarely washed and most were as foul-mouthed as they were foul-smelling. A few tried to corner her, even as skinny and unassuming as she was, but some quick thinking and agility had helped her evade them. So far.

Lana remembered a time before, when she lived with her mother and sisters. There were two, she remembered, a girl her own age who was her mirror image and a little baby, just beginning to walk. They had called the toddler Lora and her twin was named Riki. She thought of them once in a while and wondered what had become of them. The last thing she remembered was being caught in rough hands and knocked senseless.

When Lana woke days later, she was already in the Northlands. Her clothing was inadequate for the freezing temperatures and snow, and her memories were clouded by drugs. At least at first. She realized now, with years of hindsight, she'd been drugged into unconsciousness while being transported to the frozen north. Where her true homeland really lay, she did not know.

Sold into slavery, she was beaten for the first time soon after waking. Crying didn't help, and after the first few beatings, she gave in and went meekly about her tasks. She was a slave in Salomar's house, assigned first to tending the fires, then later she was given tasks that demanded more skill and strength as she grew older. She helped with the washing, sewing, cooking, and whatever needed doing.

Apparently the latest thing that needed doing was caring for a dragon egg. She'd been frightened out of her wits when Salomar threw her into the dragon's nest and locked the metal bars newly installed across the entrance to the lair. Salomar taunted that she'd be the dragonet's first meal. Fearing he was right, Lana had no choice but to make her home with the dragon egg for as long as Salomar wished it.

She tended three massive fires placed strategically around the egg, designed to keep it warm. The fires burned night and day, and for the first time since she'd been transported northward, she was completely warm. A few times when she was alone, she found herself wanting to touch the silvery, almost luminescent eggshell, but was too scared to actually do it. Still, she was tempted. One night when the guard who sat outside the barred entrance was snoring loudly, she steeled herself, went behind the egg, out of the guards' sight, and touched the iridescent shell.

A sudden, plaintive cry echoed loudly through her mind, and her hand darted back. Cautiously, she brought her fingers back to the smooth surface. Again a fear-filled cry echoed through her mind, like nothing she'd ever heard before.

Sweet Mother of All, it was the baby dragon...crying inside the egg.

It sounded so scared—almost as scared as she was—and Lana felt pity for the poor little creature.

Baby dragon, don't be afraid, she thought, instinctively placing her palm on the slightly shimmering surface of the egg. The soft mewling stopped, replaced by a feeling of cautious curiosity that somehow communicated through the shell into her mind.

Where mommy?

Sweet Mother, the baby dragon in the shell was talking to her! Marshaling her spinning thoughts, Lana tried to send a reply to the dragonet, though she'd never communicated in such a way before.

I don't know. Somehow the dragonet picked up on her thoughts. She felt its hopes deflate as it received her message. It was the most amazing thing.

Why warm then? The dragonet seemed puzzled, projecting its impressions of warmth on the three sides of its fragile home where she tended the huge fires.

I've been keeping fires lit so you would be warm, she admitted.

You new mommy?

She chuckled then. *No, I'm human, not a dragon like you.*

But you feel like me. Inside.

She had no idea what the dragonet meant, so she just shrugged. *I'll keep the fires going until you come out of your shell, then you can see what I look like. I'm very small compared to you, even now.*

You stay with me?

She felt the insecurity of the little dragon who had already been abandoned once by his mother. Lana stroked the shell with some affection though she still feared the emergence of the dragonet. In all likelihood, it would eat her as soon as it was born. But that's what Salomar wanted. That's why he'd put her in here and she wouldn't be let out until the dragonet was born and either ate her or not.

I'll stay. She sighed.

Talk to me?

I'll talk to you when I can. When the others are looking it will be hard. We are watched almost constantly, but I'll be nearby if I can't touch your shell.

Shell?

Where you are now. One day soon, I think, you'll be strong enough to break out of there.

Then we play together?

Yes, then we can play together.

If the dragonet didn't eat her first. Still, the little thing seemed eager to play and very friendly. Maybe it wouldn't eat her, and wouldn't that be a surprise to Salomar?

CRCRCR

When the first crack appeared in the egg, the guards summoned Salomar. He came with his vicious dogs to watch the emergence of the dragon. Lana tried to stay out of his line of sight as much as possible, her mind silently encouraging the little dragon who struggled with the heavy weight of the thick shell. Over the last week, the dragon had grown much stronger. She didn't even need to be in contact with the shell in order for them to communicate now. The dragon reached out to her with its young mind wherever she was and could pick up on her thoughts anywhere in the large nesting chamber.

Lana was grateful to have experienced the dragonet's friendship even for this short a time. It almost felt like having her sister back at her side. The ache of losing her twin had been constant since first awakening in the frozen north. Her sister had shared her mind on rare occasions and now this dragon was there full time. It was comforting, in its way.

The eggshell was much thicker than she thought it would be. Half a foot thick, it took all the dragonet's great strength to break through it, bit by bit. She wondered what he would look like. She knew he was male from his thoughts, but she didn't know what color he might be. She remembered hearing tales of many colored dragons from her mother when she was little, though she'd never seen one.

Now, it seemed, was her chance. Slowly, a fragile wing emerged from one side of the shell. It was so reflective in the light of the fires. At first, the shiny scales seemed to glow with every color of the rainbow, reflecting and refracting the light of the fires, but then she realized the true color of the dragonet. He was silver! Like smooth, clear, reflective ice, almost.

Oh! You're going to be so handsome!

You think so? What color?

They had talked about different colors, though the dragonet really had no concept of what color was yet. Still, he seemed curious. *You're a beautiful icy silver color, I think. Like a mirror. Very reflective and shiny. Wait 'til you see yourself.*

Soon. The baby dragon puffed. *Must rest now.*

She realized the effort it took the little dragon to get out of the armor-like shell. *Can I do anything to help you?*

No. Must do myself.

Again, she felt him mentally steeling himself for another effort. With a little mewling growl, the head of the dragonet popped through the upper portion of the huge egg. Slowly, the great diamond-like eyes blinked open, looking around the cave, then settling on her.

Mommy?

I've told you. I'm not your mommy. My name is Alania. I'm human. You're a dragon.

My name Tor.

Tor?

What mommy called me.

A tear came to her eye at the thought of this little orphaned dragon. He shouldn't be alone, but then, neither should she. Warriors had ruined both of their lives. *My mother called me Lana. It's a shorter version of my name.*

Lana. His sparkling eyes blinked down at her. *You're small.*

I told you! She smiled up at him, careful to keep her back to the bars where Salomar still watched. *I'm human. I don't have wings.*

Wings?

She spread her arms out to the sides and the dragon did the same, bursting through the shell on either side in a great shower of pearly silver. The rest of the shell fell away as baby Tor stood on shaky legs for the first time. He flapped his sticky wings, fanning the flames still roaring all around him.

The fire did nothing to tough dragon skin. Fire was his friend. In fact, the baby dragon seemed to know instinctively to polish his wings and the rest of his sticky skin in the flames.

Feels good, he said, bathing in the flames. The sight had her staring in awe. She'd had no idea dragons were so impervious to fire. Oh, she had heard as a child that they breathed flame, but she'd never thought much about it, having never met a dragon before.

When he was clean and shiny, he turned back to her, his huge head looming over her small body as he moved closer and closer. She heard the jeering yells from behind the bars. Salomar and his men were taking bets on how the dragonet would eat her. Would he play with his food or devour her quickly? The thought sickened her.

Why afraid? The dragonet's head cocked in an attitude of puzzlement.

She would be brave. If this was her last moment of life, she would face it with courage.

Are you hungry?

Yes! The dragonet's stomach growled. His head swiveled as the noise from Salomar and his men grew. The hounds barked loudly now as their jaws snapped at the bars.

You must eat to live, she said sadly.

I know.

I don't mind. She steeled herself.

Good.

Turning from her, the dragonet moved toward the bars and the snarling dogs Salomar held on long chains. The bars were meant to keep the dragonet in but were wide enough in places for the dogs to scurry through. When Salomar leapt back in fear of the approaching dragon, he loosed the chains and the dogs dashed forward.

Tor snapped at them happily, their sharp teeth and fierce growls meaning nothing to him. Within moments, all but one was eaten, the crunch of their bones deafening in the silence of the cave. The remaining dog fled the dragon and began menacing Lana. She backed away, her stomach clenching in icy-cold fear as the dog snarled at her and drew closer. Salomar had often used his dogs to savage other slaves and she knew they were used to the taste of human flesh.

Lana focused on the dog, unaware of the great silver dragonet coming up behind the beast until it was plucked from the ground in a taloned paw, run through and eaten like the others. She sighed in relief as Tor grumbled happily. When he'd finished with the dogs, Tor curled up into a sinuous ball almost at her feet and started to snore. He was sated and sleepy and, apparently, would not eat her that day.

Salomar seemed shocked at the dragon's behavior and not a little upset about losing his favorite attack dogs, but his eyes shone with avarice as he gazed at the dragon. Evidently a few dogs were less important to him than having a pet dragon at his disposal. He sent Lana a sinister smile.

"Seems he likes you. Good then. You can be his caretaker for now. If he comes to any harm, it'll be your head on a platter."

Lana trembled as the warlord stalked away, taking his minions with him. Only one guard was left to watch over them both so they wouldn't try to escape.

A reprieve, she thought. She would make good use of it. Already a plan formed in her mind. First, Tor would need to grow strong. Once he could fly and breathe fire, nothing would stand in his way. She would find a way for him to escape and maybe, just maybe, he would

14

take her along. For the first time in over a decade, things were looking up.

Chapter One

The black dragon was hurting, wounded in more than one place on his thick, ebony hide.

Sweet Mother! He'd never been in so much pain.

And the bolts kept coming.

Who knew the northern barbarians had rigged a giant crossbow they could move around so agilely? He'd taken one shot in the wing and one near his groin almost before he knew it. The bastards had more than one of the infernal machines and they were all trained on him.

Another bolt hit him in the side, its diamond-bladed tip the only thing sharp enough to slice through dragon scale. He knew he was done for, but he'd take out at least some of these sorry bastards before he fell. Turning his great head with a roar of flame, the black dragon destroyed one of the machines, frying the slovenly soldiers manning it.

He didn't have much strength left. Two of the machines remained, but he'd be lucky to attack once more, if that. He turned and swooped, and suddenly, there was a huge silver dragon beneath him, making the attack run for him. It bellowed in rage and let out a stream of fire, cooking the soldiers and the deadly machine. The silver made short work of the third crossbow as well, dodging the bolts with flying skills that would have impressed the black if he hadn't been so gravely wounded, his wings stretching painfully just to keep him aloft.

The black's eyes opened wide as he realized the sparkling silver was a fighting dragon. There was a knight on the strange dragon's back, wrapped in furs against the cold northern wind. The silver took a position underneath him and led the way to what he hoped was safety. He was too tired to think, too close to unconsciousness to question. It was good, he thought, that another of his kind was there to witness his death. Both the silver dragon and the knight would be there with him, at the end.

Not far now, brother. Tor spoke to the mind of the black dragon riding the air currents directly above him. *My rider will move forward. I want you to rest on my back as much as you can. Align your wings with mine.*

The black did as he was asked, but was clearly too far gone to answer in words. Luckily, they were close to their lair. It was just over the next mountain ridge. Tor would support the smaller black dragon, and perhaps he and Lana would have a shot at saving the black's life. Tor was lonely, being the only dragon for miles and miles around. It would be nice to have a companion of his own kind.

The black stretched his smaller wings along Tor's and his weight settled on Tor's back. It was an odd sensation, but he was big and strong and able to compensate for the added weight. Within moments, they soared over the craggy mountain ridge that kept them mostly safe from Salomar and his so-called army. Tor made the descent to the cliff-side cave as carefully as possible. It wasn't an ideal location for a lair, but it was as good as they'd been able to find on all the mountains they'd tried. They would have to move again soon, now that Salomar knew where they were, but for now, it was home.

The landing was a bit more abrupt than Tor had hoped, but then, he'd never landed with an injured dragon on his back before. The black was still semi-conscious and, once on the ground, slid to his own feet, walked a few steps into the lair, then collapsed.

Instantly, Lana was off Tor's back and at the fallen black's side. All would be well. She would help his brother of the skies.

Lana ran to the fallen dragon, her heart in her throat. She'd learned the hard way how to use her healing gift. She'd discovered it quite by accident while Tor was still newly hatched.

When he hurt himself, she was able to heal him. It was a secret she had kept hidden while they were still prisoners of Salomar, but once they escaped, she'd used her gift many times to heal Tor as he learned how to be a dragon in the wild.

He had no grown dragons to teach him, so everything he learned was either instinctive or through trial and error. Some of those errors had been very costly. Like the time he nearly ran himself through, thinking Salomar's bolts couldn't pierce dragon scale. He'd almost died that time and would have but for her gift.

Lana had learned a valuable lesson about her abilities that day too. Any major healing knocked her out completely, and though she'd saved Tor from certain death, she'd lain near death herself for several days. She learned then how she gave of her own life energy when she healed Tor. He'd watched over her recovery but was unable to do much except keep her warm with his puffing breaths and worry.

Tor made her promise, when she finally roused, to never expend herself so greatly ever again. Through trial and error, she learned how to control the healing energy until she could give just enough to keep herself conscious while still healing him as best she could. Over time, with multiple treatments of this kind, she'd healed serious wounds, many inflicted by Salomar's soldiers in their never-ending quest to get Tor back.

Now the soldiers had a new dragon to chase and Lana knew the threat to them all would triple. This striking black dragon was smaller and perhaps more easily controlled than Tor. Though only five winters old, Tor was huge, and so very strong. Salomar's soldiers tried to kill him now instead of recapture. They probably knew they had very little chance of controlling him if they did catch him, but still, every once in a while, the witch tried.

Bonded as she was with Tor's mind, Lana was well aware of Loralie's attempts to coerce him with her spells as she had his mother. Only their bond had saved him several times now. Lana was able to shake him free of the witch's spell, grounding his mind to hers in a way that defied the witch's power. She'd heard Loralie's shrieks of rage echo through the fading connection the witch had forged with Tor each time they outwitted her.

The muscular black dragon had taken three bolts, each worse than the last. Lana feared he wouldn't be flying again anytime soon, if he even survived these terrible wounds. Still, there was something very appealing about him. His faint cinnamon and clove scent appealed to her on a level she didn't quite understand.

Tor, can you remove the arrows? Gently, please.

Lana stood back to let the silver dragon work. She was too small to tug the huge bolts out of tough dragon skin, but to Tor's great strength, it was simple. She directed him to the one in the dragon's side first, moving in close to place her hands over the welling blood. It ran like a river the moment the bolt was pulled free, but when she touched his tough black hide, something magical within her stirred to life. This was very different from the usual healing response she often felt in her body and mind. This was something much, much more.

Lana gasped and nearly pulled back, but the black dragon's thick blood was pulsing dully against her fingers. He needed help and his need redirected her energy from shock to healing. She'd think about the rest later. First, she had to save him—if she could.

Using all her hard-won skill, Lana sent healing heat energy into the wound, staunching the flow of the dragon's blood and starting just a bit of the repair. She had to pace herself. There were two other wounds to close first, then she could use what remained of her energy to begin the major healing. If she had anything left.

She tried her best to ignore the familiar feeling of him. She'd never seen this dragon before, yet something inside her recognized him. Something inside her reached out to him, wanting to keep him safe, to keep him near.

Lana shook her head, moving to the bolt sticking out between the dragon's lower left leg and his body. A groin injury could be fatal, since a major artery flowed there. With great caution, she asked Tor to remove the bolt and was immediately covered in the dragon's thick blood as it spurted from the nicked artery. Lana leaned into the wound, using all her strength, sending the fire of her energies to the source of the blood flow. She panicked as it resisted her first attempts.

Lana breathed deeply and called on her energies, marshaling them and renewing her efforts. She pressed harder, both physically and with her gift, not letting up until the blood stopped flowing and the wound started to close.

"Thank the Mother," she mumbled aloud as the wounded artery sealed. The stunning black dragon had lost a lot of blood, but her magic was working. He might just pull through. She stumbled over to the last bolt, sticking out of his leathery wing, tears of strain falling unheeded down her cheeks.

"I think this one has to come out the other side. If we pull it back, the barbs will carve a hole in his wing that might never heal."

I agree. Tor positioned himself behind the black wing, supporting the bone and musculature while Lana held the wing taut. With more gentleness than anyone would credit a dragon Tor's size, he pulled the shaft through, limiting the amount of damage to the wing as much as possible. Again, she used what little remained of her energy to stop the oozing blood and begin healing. While not life-threatening, this was perhaps the worst wound, as it would severely hinder his ability to fly if it didn't heal well. Her heart nearly broke at the thought of this magnificent dragon unable to soar high where he belonged.

You need to rest. Tor's concerned voice sounded through her foggy mind. *I'll keep him warm and watch over him while you sleep.* He nudged her with his nose and Lana stumbled toward the pile of furs against the far wall. Within moments she was asleep, drained from using her gift on the strange black dragon who stirred something unknown deep in her soul.

ରଃରଃରଃ

The black dragon roused as pain pierced through the layers of unconsciousness. He blinked several times, focusing on the silver dragon who puffed warm air to keep the cave at a tolerable temperature.

Where am I?

Diamond eyes blinked open at him. They reflected every color of the rainbow. They also communicated the huge dragon's excitement.

You're awake!

Apparently so. Thank you for your assistance. I am Roland.

I'm Tor.

The silver seemed so young and eager. He didn't even blink at mention of Roland's name. That was odd enough, but he also seemed not to know what or who the black dragon was, which was odder still.

Greetings, Sir Tor. Your help was timely indeed.

Sir? What's that?

Roland was confused. *Aren't you a fighting dragon? I thought I saw a knight on your back.*

I don't know what a knight is. You saw Lana.

Lana?

The one who healed you. Or at least, began your healing. It tires her.

A female?

I suppose. She says she's human, but she feels like dragon to me, even if she looks different.

Roland filed that information away for later consideration, a sneaking suspicion forming in his mind about his rescuers.

Tor, how old are you?

The huge silver dragon paused. *I think this is my fifth winter. Lana can tell you for sure.*

Sweet Mother of All! You're just a baby. What you did to help me was amazing. Again, I thank you. Roland tried to shift and grimaced in pain. *I thought I was surely dead.*

You shouldn't move. Lana won't like it if you start bleeding again.

I won't like it either, I assure you. Roland chuckled with a dragonish snort.

Lana won't wake up for a few hours yet. Healing tires her. It almost killed her once before she learned better.

So, Roland thought to himself, an untrained healer and a giant wild dragonet. An odd combination, to be sure. He was intrigued.

Tell me where you were hatched, young Tor. Where is your mother? Your sire?

The dragonet seemed to grow anxious. *My mommy left when I was in the shell. Then Lana kept fires burning to keep me warm and she talked to me. She said she wasn't my mommy, but I love her. She helped me grow and kept me warm when Salomar wanted me to eat her! He thought I would eat Lana!* The dragonet chuckled smokily. *I ate his mean dogs instead.*

Roland knew who Salomar was. The despicable warlord thought himself king of this frozen wasteland. As far as Roland was concerned, he was welcome to it, but Salomar had recently allied himself with Skithdron and that was not to be tolerated. Now, hearing what the swine had done to this innocent wild dragonet, the list of his crimes grew. Roland vowed to make him pay for each and every one.

It was a while before I learned how to fly and breathe fire. After that, Lana and I made plans, and we finally escaped about two winters ago. They've been trying to get us back ever since.

So those huge crossbows were made for you?

Tor nodded his great head with a grim sadness. *But I learned how to fly too fast and funny for them to be able to hit me. Lana helped me practice. It's a fun game now, but the first time they hit me, I almost died. That's when Lana healed me and nearly died too.* The dragonet grew solemn once more.

But she learned better, you said. Suddenly, Roland was concerned for the small figure he could just see huddled under the covers against the far wall. *Is she all right after helping me?*

The silver head swiveled to look fondly over at his companion, his sinuous neck craning until he could breathe warm air over the small, sleeping form. *Lana is just tired. When she wakes up, she can help you more. Until then, I'll make sure Salomar can't get to you.*

You think they'll come after me?

Without a doubt. Salomar wants a pet dragon. I'm too big but he'll probably think you might be easier to control because you're smaller than me. The big head turned and peered down at him curiously. *Is that as big as you're going to get? Lana says I haven't finished growing yet. Have you?*

Roland had to laugh, the snort of dragonish amusement sending a small puff of smoke to the ceiling. *I'm fully grown, Tor. For my family, I'm large, but black dragons are usually smaller than other kinds. What we lack in size, we make up for in other ways, I like to think.*

Like how? The silver perched his huge head on his front paws, facing him.

Well, usually we're known for our flying ability. Being smaller allows us to maneuver better than some of the larger dragons.

But the arrows hit you!

Roland shook his head sadly. *That was my own stupidity, son. I didn't realize those bolts were diamond tipped. I assumed they'd bounce right off my hide.*

So did I, the first time. The younger dragon's tone was commiserating.

In my land it's illegal to hunt dragons.

Then I'd like to go there. I don't like being shot at all the time. And it would be safer for Lana. I've almost dropped her a few times.

She rides a lot?

All the time. She's my best friend. We're always together. She teaches me and sometimes she says I even teach her. I love her and she loves me.

Amazing. The black dragon shook his head softly in wonder.

Why? Don't you have human friends? Lana says not all of them are like Salomar and his soldiers.

Yes, I have many human friends and Lana is wise to tell you that many humans are good people. It's just, in my experience, it's rare for a woman to be able to speak with a dragon, much less live with one. In my land, it's usual for human males to be chosen as companions by fighting dragons. They bond and live together, training and fighting as a pair.

That's what Lana and I do. She and I hunt together and we fight Salomar's soldiers when they attack us.

If she were male, she would be a knight, Roland mused to the silver dragon though he knew the youngster didn't understand the full implications of his words.

Chapter Two

Lana woke feeling a bit more refreshed than she expected. Using her healing gift always took something out of her, but this time it felt just a little different. She sat up, keeping one of the furs around her shoulders. She wore only her thin, patched shirt and leggings. Tor kept the cave warm, but leaving a cozy pile of furs was hard for her when she first woke up. She always felt cold.

Lana relieved herself in the small pot she had fashioned from twigs and clay, then fired in Tor's hot breath. Later she would pitch the contents into a small ditch she'd dug outside their lair. For now though, she washed up with the melted snow they kept on hand inside and went to check on her patient.

The black's eyes were open and he tracked her every movement. The feel of his emerald gaze was warming in a way she couldn't define. His cinnamon-clove scent grew stronger as she neared him, bathing her senses in an odd warmth that seemed to come from within.

Can you hear me?

Yes, lady. You have my thanks.

The intimate feel of his deep voice rumbling through her mind made her twitch. She'd never shared this kind of speech with anyone but Tor. Lana moved cautiously closer to the black dragon, searching out the wounds she'd begun to heal the night before.

"I'm glad we were in time. How do you feel?"

Alive, which is more than I could have hoped for yesterday.

Lana approached him carefully. She didn't know this startlingly black dragon. Tor woke and nudged her with his nose playfully.

Roland didn't move 'cause I told him you'd be mad if he started bleeding again.

She reached up to hug the silver dragon, scratching behind his eye ridges in the way he liked. "You're a good boy, Tor."

He's not a pet. The black dragon's voice growled into her mind alone.

Lana answered him the same way. *No, he's not a pet. He's a baby. He needs love and praise.*

The black dragon backed down. *I stand corrected.*

Just who the hell are you? She faced him down with more courage than brains, considering he was much bigger than she and had the advantage of being able to breathe fire. *You should know I won't let you hurt him in any way.*

You sound like his mother.

I'm the closest thing he has to one and just as protective, so be warned.

The black dragon bowed his head stiffly. *Tor was telling me about Salomar while you slept.* His words echoed through both her mind and the dragonet's as he included the youngster in the conversation once more.

"His scouts discovered this lair two days ago. I expect they'll be back soon in force, to try to capture or kill us again, so you need to heal up quick." The black dragon grimaced as she approached, reaching out her hand to the ragged wound in his side. "I'll do my best to help you but I can't drain myself so much again in case we need to fight our way out."

I understand.

"Can you lift your wing?"

He complied and she stood under the shaky limb, examining the damage.

"Tor, sweetheart, can you help him?"

A moment later, the big silver head was under the black's wing, taking the weight off his sore and trembling muscles while the woman stepped closer. Reaching out her hands, she hummed softly, expending just a touch of her healing energy to repair the tear in his wing.

"You could probably fly on this now, but a day or two of natural healing and rest would be best." She moved to check the most painful of his injuries, the one near his groin. Again, she placed her warm little hands on the wound and again he felt the warmth of her energies bathe the area in healing. It was amazing.

When the dragonet said the woman had healed him, he'd assumed Tor meant in the traditional ways with cauterization, stitching and herbs, but this was so much more. This woman was a dragon healer!

Usually only females of the royal line had such powers. Could she be one of the lost daughters of Princess Adora of Kent, the woman recently discovered near the eastern border of his land? It seemed too impossible, yet there was little other explanation for this small woman's remarkable talent.

Her touch tickled, especially in such a sensitive area, but he was in too much pain to react to her intimate touches. She thought him an ordinary dragon. He wondered what she would think about handling him so intimately if she knew what he really was.

He watched her beautiful face, the slender feminine arches of her brows knit together in concern and concentration as she gave her all to the effort of healing him. She was so beautiful, she took his breath away. Slender and fit, she was sleekly muscled like a gazelle and just as graceful and innocent.

Her green eyes stirred him in ways he didn't fully understand as they flashed over his dragon form, assessing the damage to his tough hide. He saw intelligence spark in her gaze as she calculated how to treat him—what to tackle first and how much of her energy to expend. It was a delicate balance, he knew, for a true healer to give so freely of themselves to their patients. She was a rare and brilliant woman to have figured out so much of her talent so completely on her own.

You have a gentle touch for a self-trained healer.

She stroked the crease where his leg met his body, just barely touching the deep, angry wound there. A pulse of her healing energy shot into him, easing his pain somewhat.

"I've had a lot of practice with Tor."

The younger dragon nodded his big silver head. *I get hurt a lot.*

As do all young dragons, Roland agreed with a bit of amusement. *I was constantly in stitches when I first learned to fly.*

Stitches?

The old healer in my training Lair used to sew my wounds together with a needle and thread. Sometimes that hurt more than the wound itself.

Tor seemed to think that over. *Lana sews sometimes, but on skins for her clothes. Never on me!*

You're lucky she is a true healer, my boy. She doesn't need to use stitches. He watched as she moved back to the wound in his side. She was rationing her energy wisely this time, Roland could tell, but still she gave him all she could and it made a huge difference. Already he was in less pain and could move a bit more freely. His wing looked almost as good as new, though it was still quite sore. Still, he could fly on it if he absolutely had to. That was important with the possibility of attack at any time.

What is a training lair? Tor was proving to be a very curious boy.

Well, a Lair of any kind is a place where dragons and knights live together and train. It's usually carved into the side of a cliff so it's only reachable by flying. Inside, it's divided up into private suites for the dragons and their knights. Occasionally, mated pairs will live there, too, in larger suites to accommodate their mates and children. I trained for a while in a Lair near the royal palace when I first learned to fly.

Were you paired with a knight?

No. The black dragon shook his head. *I will never do so. Black dragons are different from other dragons, Tor. We not only fight with the dragons and knights, we lead them. I and my brothers each lead factions of our kingdom's armies of fighting dragons and their knights.*

So there are lots of dragons where you come from?

Oh yes. Many hundreds. They are the protectors of the land and partners with the humans who live there.

Is it very far away?

A few days flight over the mountains to the south.

The huge silver head swiveled to the woman. *Lana, can we go there? I don't think Salomar could find us there.*

I can guarantee he won't. It's illegal to intentionally hurt a dragon in my land. You would be welcome there, Tor. As would Lana. The ability to heal dragons is a rare and wondrous gift.

Lana sat back, resting familiarly on Tor's bent knee. "I've been wanting to leave the Northlands but I didn't know where we could go."

I can lead you away from here and to my land. You'll both be safe there.

She turned to the silver dragon, hugging his long neck loosely. "Do you really want to go? It would be a long journey."

I want to go, Lana. I can fly a long time. You know that.

She laughed and kissed his nose. "You fly longer and longer each day, Tor, and if you get any bigger we won't fit in this cave!"

He is big for his age, isn't he?

"I only saw Tor's mother once before Salomar and his witch ran her off, but she was huge. I think he's nearly her size now so I guess he'll stop growing soon."

You're going to be a mighty dragon when you're fully grown, Tor. I know you would do well in my land.

"Then we'll go with you when you're ready to fly." Lana's voice was a little frightened, but firm. Roland rejoiced silently at how easy it was to convince them. Now all he had to do was heal enough to fly home. The sooner, the better.

ଔଔଔ

Roland contemplated when to reveal his true nature to the petite beauty who kept fussing over his injuries when the attack came. Pain kept him awake while both the woman and the young dragon slept, and it was a good thing. For it was Roland's sharp hearing that alerted him to the fur-clad soldiers making their way toward the mouth of the cave.

Lana, Tor, wake up. Don't make a sound. We have company.

Where?

The beauty was already slipping from the furs, crouched with a rough blade in her hand that should have been much too big for her small body. But the sleek muscles in her arms said she knew how to swing a sword and Tor had told him how she scrounged their few belongings from the soldiers they had felled. The dragonet had told him how Lana had taught herself how to defend them both as best she could.

They're on the slope just in front of the cave opening. They're trying to set traps, I think.

Can you fly?

If I must, and I think we must. Get your pack and get on Tor's back as quietly as you can. I'll move up to the opening and block the light. They can't see past my black hide, I'll bet.

Good thinking. Tor's silver scales reflect even the smallest amount of light. That's why they come at night.

Sneaky bastards.

Roland moved up to just behind the mouth of the cave, watching the enemy soldiers. They didn't see him, he was sure. There were advantages to having a black hide.

How are we going to do this?

Roland liked that the woman deferred to his expertise without even realizing she did so. Over the past hours she'd come to trust him just a little. On some instinctual level she recognized him, as he did her.

Are you two ready?

Yes, Roland. Tor sounded eager and just a bit nervous.

Good. Tor, I want you to wait for my signal. I'm going to torch the hillside where they're setting traps for us. When it's clear, I want you to take to the sky as fast and as high as you can without dropping Lana. Can you do that?

I can, Roland. I can do that.

Good. Now just give me a minute to get into position.

Roland timed his blast as best he could. He breathed in deep, preparing to flame the humans and their traps. He let loose with a mature roar of fire, incinerating everything within fifty yards of the cave entrance. There was plenty of room for the young dragon to escape while the flames roared high. His silver wings protected his rider from the heat and flame as he roared into the sky, the black dragon following close behind.

Roland kept himself between the big silver and the ground, hoping to mask the glinting sparkle of his wings as much as possible from the hunters below. It seemed to be working, but Roland was tiring far faster than he'd hoped. They cleared the first mountain and were nearing the second peak when Roland made a rough landing on a craggy spire of rock. There was a small ledge, just big enough for two dragons. Tor circled and finally landed when Roland did not rise again.

Are you all right?

Tor's young voice sounded through Lana's mind though she knew he addressed the black dragon, panting on the ground. She jumped off Tor's back and went to Roland, her hands outstretched to stop the new flow of blood from the wound in his side.

I will be. I just need to rest.

Can't stay here, though. It's too cold up here for Lana.

Between the two of us, we will keep her warm enough for tonight. This is the safest place for us right now. There's no way Salomar's men can climb up here after us.

Tor seemed to consider. *You're right! You're smart, Roland.*

33

The black dragon chuckled while Lana worked on his wound. She was tiring fast, giving him a great deal of her energy, but he really needed her help.

"It's not as bad as I'd feared. You need to rest though, and this place is a good one. I'll make do with the furs."

If you can drag that dead wood over here, I'll start a fire for you. They won't see it way up here and even if they do, there's nothing they can do about it.

Lana smiled and made a dash for a good-sized, fallen pine log, but it was too heavy for her. Tor saved her the work by plucking it up in one talon and dropping it neatly in front of the black dragon. She scooted out of the line of fire, and within moments, Roland gave her a roaring fire that would last a few hours at least. She made a bed for herself from the few furs she'd managed bring with them in her travel pack.

Come here, Roland told her quietly, *closer to me. I'll keep you warm.*

Lana shook her head and laughed. "No, thanks. Tor has nearly squashed me too many times for me to sleep near a dragon ever again."

I promise I won't move a muscle. I'm fully grown, Lana. I do have some control over myself, contrary to when I was Tor's age. He'll learn to settle down as soon as his bones stop aching from the growth spurts.

"So that's why…"

When dragons are his age, they are growing fast, particularly while asleep. The bones ache slightly as they expand and movement is the only way to relieve it. He doesn't even know he's doing it. It's instinctive.

"There's so much I don't know about dragons."

You've done very well with him for a novice, Lana. Your love has guided him. That's the most important thing. He has a kind heart, even after all he's been through.

Lana couldn't respond around the lump in her throat. She moved her furs closer to the black dragon and jumped slightly when he raised his good wing over her head. It was starting to snow lightly.

Under here, Lana. I promise I won't hurt you and you'll be warm and safe while you sleep.

Lana was skeptical, but it really was freezing at this altitude. She could barely feel her feet as it was. Snuggling into the furs, she allowed Roland to wrap his good wing around her, tucking her into his side. He was right. It was toasty warm next to his hot body and the snow sizzled into steam as it touched the wing over her head. She looked out on the snowy sky, the small fire burning steadily in front of her, and realized, in that quiet moment, she was comfortable and completely warm for the first time in years.

"You're a good dragon, Roland. Thank you. After I sleep a bit, I'll try another treatment on your side. I'm too tired now."

That's all right, little one. Sleep now. We'll worry about everything else in the morning.

Roland dozed, careful of the woman at his side. She felt right, cuddled next to him. She unconsciously stroked his flank with her face and hair as she moved slightly, her hands coming to rest in the ticklish spot just where his wing met his body, but he didn't move. He liked the feel of her small, gentle hands on him. Perhaps too much.

He became aware of warmth seeping from her into him that should not be. Taking quick stock, he realized she was reaching out to him with her healing ability, even in sleep.

Lana, sweetling, wake up. You have to stop trying to heal me. I don't want you wearing yourself out on my account. It could be dangerous.

"What?" Her voice was drowsy, still half-asleep as her hands subtly stroked him.

Pull your power back, little one. Do not expend your healing energy like this.

"But I'm not doing anything."

You are. I feel it, Lana.

"No." She faced him, coming out from under the shelter of his wing to meet his gaze. "I feel no power drain."

But I feel your heat. The heat of your healing power.

"That can't be."

Roland remembered then, a legend of his family. It didn't seem possible that this little, unexpected woman could hold the powers his family had thought lost for generations, but then, stranger things had happened since he'd flown north. This would require a great deal of thought on his part and he didn't want to trouble her with the magnitude of the discovery until he was certain.

It's all right, sweetling. Go back to sleep. I must have been mistaken.

She moved back under his wing, settled back against him and was soon asleep once more. Roland watched carefully, gauging the energies flowing once more from her to him and back again. He knew then he wasn't mistaken. Relaxed and out of immediate danger, they were feeding off each other in an endless loop. Neither would suffer ill effects from this kind of innate healing, or so the legends held. This was a rarity among rarities. No pair had formed this kind of bond in centuries, but it seemed this big-hearted, self-trained healer was doing so. It was a miracle. Or perhaps, he thought with a dragonish snort, it was magic.

Chapter Three

"You're much better this morning." Lana moved constantly, trying to stay warm as she examined the worst of Roland's injuries. He loved the feel of her little hands, so gentle on his hide. "I thought you did a lot more damage than this when you blasted out of the cave."

So did I, but I guess we got lucky. I feel fit to fly, as long as we take it easy.

Tor bounded over, pushing snow everywhere. *How long will it take us to get to your land now?*

A few days, I think, but it'll be warmer as soon as we clear the mountains. I hope we can do that by tomorrow afternoon.

"So only one more night of snow?" Lana's teeth chattered as she ran her hand down to his groin injury. He did his best to concentrate on anything but her tender touch in his most private areas.

If you're lucky. There may be snow on the ground in the foothills as well, but it won't be quite this cold.

Lana sneezed daintily as she stepped back from him and moved to his side. "I'm almost done for now. I think you'll be fine as long as you take it as easy as possible. No acrobatics, all right?"

Yes, mother.

Lana chuckled as Tor laughed and played in the snow. Roland could easily see she'd been a good mother to the orphaned dragonet. He was happy and his innocent heart was full of laughter and fun, as it should be. After hearing what they'd both been through at the hands of Salomar, he knew it could have turned out quite differently.

Roland felt the tingling heat in his sore side and then the easing of his pain, accompanied by her expenditure of energy. She leaned against him a moment and he pulled his good wing around to steady her.

Are you all right?

"That's what I should be asking you."

You're swaying on your feet. You need to stop feeding me all your energy, Lana. We have a long flight ahead of us.

"Not too long, I hope."

I promise I'll stop when I need to stop.

She straightened in the embrace of his warm, enveloping wing. "All right then. That's about all I can do for now. Make frequent stops, Roland, and I'll check you over each time we land."

They did not encounter any more of Salomar's men on their way out of the mountains, though Roland moved much slower than he would have wished. Still, he found them a secure perch for the night and the temperature, while still well below freezing, was just a touch warmer the farther south they flew.

Lana curled up at his side again, seeking his warmth and sharing her energy with him unconsciously as she slept. It was a different sort of energy—one that wouldn't drain her—or he would have put a stop to it. She gave so much of herself to heal his grave wounds when she was awake, he wouldn't stand for her doing the same while asleep. But this was different. This was an exchange of energy on a whole other level. She fed from his vast strength as she returned healing energy to him. He powered her and she healed him. It was slow, but it was definitely beneficial.

When he woke in the morning to find her tucked against his side, he felt much, much better. Roland liked the feel of her close to him, sharing his warmth, and he realized he just plain liked her. A lot. After waking like a sleepy kitten next to his warm body, she examined him, giving of her own energy in the only way she had known to this point, to help speed his healing even more.

They reached the foothills by afternoon and were able to fly lower, where the air was warmer. Tor enjoyed the comparatively warm updrafts, frolicking like the enormous child he was as Roland looked on with indulgence. Riding securely on his back as if she'd been born a knight, Lana screeched and laughed with her young friend, enjoying every swoop and dive the agile youngster put her through.

Roland was getting stronger too, but it was slow going. Without Lana and her care, he would have died of his wounds, so grievous they had been. Recovery was going amazingly fast with Lana's attentions, but he was still not in the best shape. He had them stop on a grassy hill, only partially covered with dots of snow so he could rest. Tor pounced on a rabbit for Lana's lunch and Roland obliged by lighting a fire in the kindling she gathered so she could cook the rabbit to her liking.

Tor ambled off to hunt and brought back a wild goat for him. Roland tore into it with hunger. He realized, only then, it had been days since he'd eaten. While dragons could survive for weeks when necessary without food, it wasn't easy, and though raw mountain goat wasn't his favorite dish, it would do in a pinch.

He polished off the goat while Lana daintily ate the rabbit she'd cooked, throwing the bones and bits she didn't want to Tor. They were a good team, he realized, recognizing the habits of old friends who had a familiar routine.

We could stay here tonight, Roland sent the thought to his companions.

Lana shrugged. "I could do with a rest and the fire is nice."

It won't keep you warm all night, though.

She smiled up at him. "But you will, won't you? I like sleeping at your side, Roland. It's like sleeping next to a furnace."

I like it too, little Lana. You are welcome in my bed anytime. Only Roland knew the full implication of his words, but the time was coming when he would reveal himself to her. Soon.

She laughed and settled her small pack on the ground, setting up her version of camp. It was sparse—just a few furs she'd managed to pack into her bags when she realized they would have to leave the cave. Thanks to Roland's warning, she'd had time to grab the bags on her way out of the lair, so she had a few of her meager possessions.

She'd kept a lot of her smaller items in a bucket that had been scrounged from somewhere. It seemed to be one of her most prized possessions for she treated it carefully when she used it to fetch water from the nearby stream. Roland was still too sore in his side and groin to walk much on land, so she set pail after pail of water in front of him until his thirst was sated.

Roland watched her with his keen dragon sight as she peeled off one layer of clothing at a time down by the small stream. She washed economically, used to washing one part of her supple body at a time because it was so cold where she lived. It wasn't too much warmer here, but it was better.

Roland idly wondered what she would think of the heated baths in his Lair. Would she dive in, her graceful body gloriously naked and revel in the ability to wash her whole body at once? Or would she be afraid of the water, since it was doubtful she knew how to swim? Either way, he would enjoy showing her his home's amenities and seeing more of the lithe, feminine form he could only really guess at, though what he could see, a piece at a time, piqued his interest greatly.

Roland felt strong stirrings of desire that should have been blocked by the immense pain of his wounds, but the desire wasn't of the body alone. It was a stirring near his heart that was totally unfamiliar. He wanted to pamper this poor girl, dress her in the finest silks and satins and let her play free from worry and fear. He wanted to cherish her.

And he wanted to fuck her. There was no denying it, but his body had to heal first. He stayed in dragon form because these wounds—even half-healed as they were—would have killed his human body. A day or two more, he figured, and it would be safe to shift. Then he would take her in his human arms and kiss her with his human lips. He would take her and make her his own.

Lana slept well and awoke refreshed. Roland's injuries looked much better this morning and she thought black dragons must heal in their sleep even better than regular dragons like Tor. They flew far that day, resting less often, and she realized Roland took breaks more for her and Tor's convenience than his own. He seemed so much more powerful, so much better. She was happy to see it.

At one point, he trumpeted loudly and landed on a rocky outcropping. Tor followed suit.

From here you can see my land, he said with a touch of pride. *See the river in the distance? That is the Arundelle River and it marks the northernmost boundary of the Kingdom of Draconia and the Northland wastes. We should reach*

41

the river by nightfall if we push hard, but I think perhaps it would be wiser to spend the night on this side of the border and cross in the morning.

"Why is that?" she asked, stretching her limbs a bit.

The border is guarded. A strange dragon such as Tor will be welcomed, but challenged when they first sight him. You, milady, will be a shock to the knights, for no female has partnered with a dragon, as you have with Tor, in millennia. I want to rest up and see this in the full light of day.

His tone indicated amusement and some deviltry. Lana raised one eyebrow in his direction, but he only chuckled in that dragonish way of his.

"Very well, Roland. We follow where you lead."

Roland stopped them for the night near a tributary of the huge river that had grown larger and larger the closer they flew throughout the day. Lana remarked to him each time they stopped at how large the river was and he could tell it was the biggest body of water she had ever seen. He thought of showing her the ocean and looked forward to the light of wonder it would no doubt put in her eyes. There were so many wonders this beautiful little woman had never seen. He would show them all to her, but first she had to know who and what he truly was.

He would deal with the "who" later, but for tonight, he had plans to show her exactly what he was. One more night of their unconscious power exchange would make him well enough to shift without danger, he guessed. It would have to be. Before the next dawn he planned to show her the truth of his form and explain a little more about black dragons and her connection to the line. Hopefully she would take it well.

Roland directed them to a special area of the river he'd visited before. There were a series of small pools on this side of the border that would act as bathing pools and provide fresh drinking water for them all without Lana having to tug the heavy pail over to him time after time.

Roland landed almost perfectly, having to limp only a few feet to a small pool where he could easily crane his long neck over to drink. He drank thirstily, noting Tor doing the same at another of the little pools while Lana set up her tiny camp.

Tor suddenly jumped back, landing in another pool with a huge splash, drenching them all. The look of surprise on his young face overtook the shock of the water.

"What is it, Tor?" Lana's voice was concerned as she moved toward her dragonet.

Something moved in the water!

Roland laughed with relief, realizing it was probably a fish that had startled the youngster. He reached in carefully with one talon and neatly speared a large fish from the bottom of his own pool. He held it up to the light, the scales shining iridescently in the fading sun as it wriggled furiously in death.

Have you never seen one of these before?

What is it? Tor moved closer to examine the odd creature, his eyes wide.

"I think..." Lana said hesitantly. "I think it's a fish. Am I right?"

Right you are, milady. Roland dropped the fish at her feet, turning back to pluck a few more out of the pool. He threw one to Tor and started crunching on the others himself. After he had quickly eaten three and taken the edge off his hunger, he turned back to them.

At last, I get to provide dinner for my rescuers. Let this be the first of many. Roland bowed his great head to the fish at Lana's feet. *Allow me to prepare and cook this for you, milady. I think you'll like it.*

"I remember fish." Her voice held the edge of tears and a bit of wonder. "My mother would make them sometimes with butter and herbs when we lived near a stream. They were smaller than that though."

Roland listened with compassion in his heart while he used his sharp claws to filet the big fish. He threw the innards to the younger dragon who was now chasing fish in the larger pool somewhat successfully. For every fish Tor caught, five got away, but he was chuckling with the effort and enjoying the game as one his age should.

Using just a hint of his own flame, Roland cooked the fish to perfection before handing it back to Lana, using the large pad of his paw, between the deadly talons, as a kind of platter.

Try this, he coaxed as she stepped hesitantly forward.

She plucked a piece of the tender, cooked fish from his extended palm and put it to her lips. Her little tongue licked it first, making him think things about that tongue that were better saved for when he was in his alternate form. Blissfully unaware of his salacious thoughts, she took the piece of fish into her mouth and started to chew delicately. Her eyes lit up and tears formed there, surprising him. She was such a strong little thing, it was a shock to see her tender feelings so exposed.

"I remember this! It tastes like I remember."

Just without the butter and herbs.

She laughed at his dry observation and took the rest of the cooked fish from him, placing it on a small slate she used as a plate. She ate the whole thing with relish, savoring every bite as her eyes glazed with memories. Roland watched her, enjoying her delight in such a simple thing. He would give her many such happy moments, he vowed. He would bring her new experiences and shower her with gifts of every kind. He wanted to see her happy. It was a need he had that was so foreign, it was startling, but it just felt right. She was his. He would pamper her and give her everything within his power to make her happy. She just didn't know it yet.

Finishing the meal, Lana wiped her mouth daintily with a small cloth she used to clean and then wrap her few belongings. Everything was soaked from Tor's earlier splashing but it was warmer here in the lowlands. Tor continued to play in the nearby pools, showering them from time to time as he caught or lost a fish. He was enjoying himself immensely, learning a new skill, and catching a healthy dinner at the same time.

"Thank you, Roland." Lana's eyes glowed up at him. "I'd forgotten fish, and I think you're an even better cook than my mother was." She laughed up at him and he chuckled with a dragonish snort of smoke at her little joke.

I'm glad I could give that memory back to you, little one. I like to see you happy.

He touched her gently with his muzzle, rubbing over her soft breasts and relishing the feel of her arms as they came up to hug him like she often did with Tor. It wasn't something most dragons welcomed from humans, but then, he wasn't most dragons. He was only half-dragon. The other half of him longed to feel her wrap her arms around him in passion, but that would come soon. As soon as he could manage it.

"I'd better clean up. It's so warm, I think I'll take this opportunity to wash everything, since Tor's already helped get all my belongings wet. Plus, I don't want to look like a dirty Northerner when your people see us tomorrow."

They'll be amazed by you no matter how you look.

He watched her move around gracefully, dipping to gather up her few belongings and take them to the side of one of the smaller pools. She began to wash everything and he uncovered some big rocks for her, which he heated with his breath to a nice warm temperature so she could lay her furs and extra clothing out to dry.

"Why is it such a big deal that Tor and I are friends?"

It's a rare woman who can communicate with dragons. It's even rarer for anyone to be able to heal dragons with their touch. I know of only a few people in the whole kingdom who have the gift. He paused, considering his next words carefully. *I think you should know about two women in particular, who were recently discovered to have the same gift. The ability to heal dragons is an inherited trait of royal blood. Our long-ago king, Draneth the Wise, made a pact between dragons and humans that keeps my land peaceful and secure, both races living in harmony. These two women were lost members of the House of Kent, a line of royal blood distantly related to the current king's line. I think you may also be part of the House of Kent.*

"But I'm not royal. At least, I don't think I am. I have no idea really, but before I was taken north, we lived simply. Not at all how I imagine a royal would live."

You might be surprised. The two women I mentioned? They lived in hiding and did not even know of their birthright until just a short while ago. I believe you may be related to them.

Lana stood from the stream, her clothing wet in patches, her expression deadly serious, her face pale.

"Do you know their names?"

Why?

"I remember my sister. Two sisters, actually. We were little, but my sister was my mirror image. I called her Riki. And the baby, she was just a toddler. We called her Lora." Tears fell unheeded down her face as she shared just a tiny bit of her past with him. Hope she didn't dare voice shone in her eyes.

He moved closer and faced her straight on. *The younger of the women is named Belora and her mother is called Adora.*

"Mother? Stars!" Lana fell to her knees on the soft bank, her body trembling. Roland puffed warm air to comfort her, wishing he could transform and take her into his arms, but it was still too soon. "I don't know my mother's name, but Belora could be baby Lora. My name is Alania but Mama always called me Lana."

Then you are most likely one of the twin daughters of Adora we have been seeking.

"Seeking?"

Once we realized who Adora and Belora were—long-lost cousins of the king—we sent word to all dragons and knights in the land and beyond to search for word of Adora's lost twin daughters.

"I don't know if I'm really one of the girls you're looking for, but I'd like to meet these women and see if they know me, or if I recognize them. But it's been so long!"

Roland limped over, caging her with his strong forelegs, his heat reaching out to her. *I will take you to them myself. I have few doubts that you are one of the twins we seek. Your healing gift and your relationship with Tor are proof enough for me.*

Chapter Four

Lana reached out for Roland, drained emotionally and needing to cling to his strength. In just a few short days this strange black dragon had become a guide through unknown lands, a protector and a close friend. And now he was giving her hope that she might find her family after all this time. It was enough to make her cry, and she never cried. Well, at least not often. She'd learned early on in Salomar's household that crying was a waste of effort and only brought unwanted attention.

Roland's emotional strength was even greater than Tor's. Roland was fully grown, for one thing, and emotionally mature. He was also willing to let her lean on him while her emotions rocked from one extreme to the other. There was something so comforting about his nearness. She had slept better these last few nights, nestled under his protective wing, than she ever had in her life. He felt so good to her. So right.

"Can Tor and I stay with you, at least for a little while, when we get to your home? I mean, is there room for us?"

Yes, little one. There will always be room for you and Tor wherever I am. You are my saviors and my good luck charms. I won't let you leave me ever again.

She leaned against his broad chest, hugging his long neck. "That sounds so nice, but what if this woman Adora really is my mama? Oh, sweet Mother of All! Roland, thank you so much for telling me about them. They might really be my family."

I think they probably are. And if I'm right, we'll go where they are or ask them to come to us. I know they'll want to see you as much as you'll want to see them.

"Oh, I hope you're right!"

I'm always right. You'll learn that soon enough. His tone was teasing as his neck craned over her to breathe warmth into the pool she'd been using to wash her things. *You're shivering, Lana. Warm yourself in the pool and finish your washing. We need to rest up so we can cross the river at first light. I want the dawn to sparkle off Tor's beautiful silver scales so you make a grand entrance to my land. His size alone will have all the dragons talking about him soon enough, but we have few silver dragons among our number and none so brilliant as Tor.*

Is that true? Tor bounded over, full of fish and starting to get sleepy as young dragonets often did. *Are there other dragons who look like me?*

A few, Roland told him. *But none as big as you are, Tor, I don't think. The dragons in my land are all the colors of the rainbow. There are only a handful of black like me. A few dozen are silver, but they are mostly silvery gray—not bright, clear, iridescent silver like you. If I had to guess, I'd say you were an Ice Dragon. They are rare, even in the Northlands.*

An Ice Dragon? That sounds nice, was Tor's sleepy reply as he settled his large bulk down for a nap. Within moments, he was fast asleep.

Lana smiled fondly at him as she made her way to the small pool Roland had heated for her. She took off her footwear and tested the water with her toes, a little hesitant about how deep the water might be. Cautiously, she stepped into the shallow part of the pool where she could still see the bottom, moving inch by inch lower into the warm water. It felt like heaven.

Her filthy pants and tunic billowed around her as she sank lower and she decided to take them off once she was in water up to her shoulders. Turning toward the bank, she found a good spot with a big, flat rock and a shallow area where she washed her clothes, then wrung them out as best she could. She threw the damp clothing toward the grassy bank where Roland's warm breath made quick work of everything that had gotten wet.

Lana noticed the black dragon watching her intently. She realized she was naked under the water, but this was a dragon. He should have no interest in her naked human body, but something gleaming in the depths of his faceted emerald eyes made her think otherwise. Ridiculous, she told herself, he's a dragon.

Why the blushes, little one? Roland's voice echoed in a low purr through her mind as his head dipped lower and closer to the pool where she stood submerged to her shoulders.

"Stop looking at me like that."

Like what?

"Like you want to eat me."

Roland chuckled in his dragonish way, sending smoke billowing lightly near her head. *But what if I said, I did want to eat you?*

She sank lower into the pool, her eyes wide. "I thought you said your land was civilized. Civilized to me means dragons don't eat humans."

What if I weren't a dragon? At least not completely.

"What in the world are you talking about?"

I will tell all tomorrow, little one. For now, rest assured my land is civilized and you will be safe and welcome there.

She was truly confused by his words and the speculative tone in his voice. Roland backed off though, setting his large head on his front paws, watching her as she began to relax again. He sent puffs of his hot, cinnamony breath over her to keep her warm in the chill night air. The last rays of the sun were just beginning to fade. It would be dark soon.

You had better come out of there before you wrinkle like a raisin.

"What's a raisin?"

It amazed him how such simple things had been denied this beautiful soul, when he'd been raised with such bounty. The idea humbled him.

A raisin is a dried grape.

"What's a grape?"

She stroked the cooling water up and down her arms as she scrubbed her skin with some of the tall grass growing by the pond. It was scrubweed, common in many areas of the world and, apparently, she remembered well enough the use of it from her childhood.

A grape is a kind of fruit. They grow in bunches in the southern regions and have a sweet, juicy taste. You'll like them. When they're dried, they wrinkle up, very much like your skin is wrinkling from staying in the water so long.

"But it feels so good to get clean!" The smile on her face was so refreshing he could hardly condemn her for lolling in the waters he kept warm for her.

At the Lair they'll have bathing chambers with heated spring water that you don't have to share with fish and frogs. He snorted with a chuckle as a tiny frog hopped up onto the bank near his foot. *There will be scented oils and perfumed soaps and special herbal formulations for your beautiful hair to make it shiny and smooth.*

Her eyes gazed at him in wonder. "It sounds wonderful, but will they let me use such grand things?"

Of course! You are my guest and more than that, you are a gentlewoman in your own right, companion to an Ice Dragon the likes of which my land has not seen in many, many years. Lana, do not doubt yourself or your worth. You are a beautiful, intelligent, talented woman and you will be welcome in my land and in my home.

"When you say it that way, I almost believe it. But I'm not used to anything but working, running, fighting and hiding, Roland. It's hard to get used to the idea that Salomar can't try to hurt us anymore."

Never again. He drew his head up high and stiff with anger at the thought of what this beautiful girl had been through in her young life. *Neither Salomar, nor any like him, will ever threaten you or Tor again. Not as long as I breathe. You have my word on that, Lana, and you will learn that once given, my word is my oath.*

She tried to wipe away a tear so he wouldn't notice, but he saw her furtive movement. She was coping as best she could with all the changes in the past few days, he knew. What she needed now was to feel safe. His voice was much gentler as he settled his massive head back down on the ground before her, his warm breath puffing in her direction.

Now come on out of there. I'll keep you warm, sweetheart.

"I'm so glad Tor and I found you when we did."

No happier than I, he rumbled. *I owe you my life.*

She smiled at him, blushing just a little. "It was Tor that got you to safety. He's the one who saved you."

But you're the one who healed me. Without both of you, I would have been dead. I owe you both a life debt, as the wandering Jinn would say. Taking you to the safety of my homeland is the very least I can do.

She started forward in the water, making his breath catch internally as her skin was revealed little by little from the cloaking water. "We'll be happy to be safe for the first time in Tor's life. He's never known peace."

Roland tried to concentrate on her words, but it was no use. He watched her as she drew closer to the bank, every last coherent thought wiped from his mind.

Like the goddess rising from the ocean, Lana walked up out of the small pool, her skin gleaming pink in the final rays of the setting sun. She was the image of womanly perfection to him. Generous breasts with pouting nipples, sleek muscles from years of living hard, a trim waist and rounded hips, she was as beautiful as he had known she'd be. Naked, she stood before him and he was completely mesmerized.

Then she giggled.

"Will you dry me off, Roland? Please?"

He perked up, realizing belatedly that he'd been staring while his thoughts roamed over her delectable body. He had to remember she thought he was only a dragon.

Of course, milady. Just a second.

He took a deep breath and sighed a warm wind over her front, blowing the wet strands of her gorgeous, fiery hair back as the water droplets clinging to her skin melted away before his heat. She turned around and he had to pause for a moment to catch his breath at the beautifully pert, round ass presented so innocently before him. She looked back at him over her shoulder curiously, and he sent the warm breeze of his exhalation over her back. Her supple spine and the mass of flaming auburn hair shone with coppery licks of fire in the red rays of the dying sun.

You are so beautiful, Lana.

She smiled as she turned back to him. "I'm glad you think so, but I'm rather plain for a human, I'm sure."

She bent to her tunic which was mostly dry and slipped it over her head, forgoing trousers since they weren't dry enough to wear just yet. Having eaten and washed, she was yawning when she bent to check Roland's wounds. At all costs he had to keep her from checking his groin. After seeing her beautiful nudity, even his healing dragon body had gotten quite obviously excited. He didn't want to have to try to explain why a dragon would get hard at the sight of a beautiful human woman. Not yet at least.

You're tired, Lana. Come here. He held up his wing, hoping she would take the invitation to rest warmly, safely away from the inexplicable evidence of his arousal.

With a last pulse of healing energy to his side, she covered her yawning lips with one dainty hand and nestled down under his wing. She was asleep almost before she settled fully against him. Roland sighed in relief. Tomorrow he would tell her his secret and see how she reacted to the very real *human* male holding her safe and warm in his arms.

Roland woke Lana just before dawn when the pearly gray light grew bright enough for human eyes to see. Tor was still fast asleep and Roland knew the young dragon would sleep on for at least an hour or more. Now came the moment of truth for Roland...and his lady.

Lana? Sweetheart, wake up. There's something I have to tell you.

Is it morning yet? She yawned, answering him in the quiet of her mind as she rubbed her eyes, coming awake slowly like a newborn kitten. He loved that about her. Her innocent femininity was just one of the many facets of her that inspired new, tender emotions in his heart.

Nearly. Lana, there's something important you have to know.

She looked over at him and he knew she was coming fully awake.

What is it? Is something wrong?

No, nothing's wrong. There's just a secret I need to share with you and you can't tell Tor. He's too young yet to keep this secret, and secret it must remain—at least for now.

Her expression grew troubled. *I don't hide things from Tor.*

For the safety of my kingdom, you must hold this one secret close to your heart for a short while. More than just my own life depends on it.

Then why in the world do you want to tell me?

You'll understand when you see... He blew out a hot, frustrated breath. *Oh hell, just watch.*

Lana gaped in awe as the black wing around her transformed into a muscular, *human* arm. She nearly shrieked when, instead of a black dragon, she was being held close to the hot body of a tall warrior clad in tight-fitting, black leather breeches and little else.

"Sweet Mother of All!" Her whispered words were caught by powerful, male lips as he captured her mouth with his in the first kiss she had ever known. It was hot and sweet, faintly smoky and pure. Something inside her shifted as the incredibly handsome man laid her back on the soft grass, hovering over her small body with his large, muscular form.

"Do you understand now?" His words sounded near her ear as he pulled slightly back. Dark green human eyes watched her carefully, a slight smile playing about the hard lips that had just kissed her breathless.

"Roland?"

He nodded. "In the flesh."

"But how?"

"I'm of the royal bloodline, Lana. All the males of my line are both human and dragon. Black dragons, to be precise. Only the royal blacks can change form from human to dragon at will. It's part of our heritage, part of our birthright, part of the agreement between human and dragonkind to peacefully coexist as they coexist in the males of my line."

She ran one hand over the sharp angles of his face, marveling at how the dragon resembled the man. Though in completely different form, she recognized him. He was not a stranger to her. And he was so good-looking, he took her breath away.

His green eyes sparkled just like the emerald dragon eyes she had come to know so well over the past days. The arch of his eyebrow was so similar in shape and angle to the eye ridge of the dragon. The curve of his cheek was in the same proportion as the angular jaw of the dragon.

"You *are* Roland." Her voice was a breathless whisper of awe as her eyes lit up with discovery. She gasped as another thought occurred. "Sweet Mother! Are you a prince or something?"

His smile deepened, revealing sexy dimples. "Or something. You'll find out all the grisly details when we get to the palace and meet my family, I'm sure."

"You're taking me to the palace?" The thought struck fear into her heart.

"If I'm right, you too are a member of one of the royal bloodlines. You must learn about your heritage and claim your birthright, Lana. By right of your birth, you're also part of the royal court."

"Are we related?" Apprehension filled her.

Roland nodded, confirming her fears. "Yes, sweet, but only very distantly. The House of Kent, to which I suspect you belong, and my line are quite far apart, but both our lines breed true. Which means you're half-dragon too. It's your gift to heal dragons, as do most of the women of the royal lines."

"Half-dragon?"

He chuckled, kissing her nose. "Yes, little one. It's probably the only reason you were able to claim and tame a great northern Ice Dragon. Such a feat is not easily done. Did you never wonder why you were the only person in Salomar's household who could speak with your dragonet?"

"But I wasn't the only one."

"What?" His dark eyes grew alert, his expression questioning.

"He has a witch." Lana's heart pounded as she remembered the evil woman. "Her name is Loralie. She's tried to lure Tor from me many times. She's the one who sent his mother away with no memory of the egg she left behind."

"When we get to the palace, you must tell my brothers everything you know about this witch."

She nodded, sensing how important this was to him. "I'll gladly tell you everything I know about Salomar's household if it will help you defeat him."

"Defeat him? What do you know of his plans?" A cunning smile broke over his face.

She smiled back. "I didn't spend all my time languishing in dark, cold caves. As much as his men hunted us, Tor and I harried them. We intercepted messengers and waylaid enough scouts to know he plans to bring war on a kingdom to the south with his allies in the east. I can only guess that the kingdom he intends to move against is yours."

Roland drew back from her, rising to sit back on his haunches, his expression hard. "I suspected as much, which is why I flew north. I wanted to do a little reconnaissance. Instead I almost died."

"You didn't know about the weapons he's developed to fight dragons."

He turned back to her with a bright light in his eyes. "But you do. You know all about his tactics and his weapons. He's been testing and perfecting them on you and Tor."

She sat up, nodding slowly as she realized what he was getting at. "Yes, you're probably right." She took his hand in hers. "We'll tell you everything we know and though I can't speak for Tor, I will fight with you against Salomar to the best of my ability. If ever a man deserved to die, it's him. Deliberately orphaning a beautiful baby like Tor is just one of his crimes, but that's the one that hurts me the most."

Roland reached out with his muscular arms and pulled her close. "You have a kind and brave heart, Lana. We'll keep Tor safe and see he grows up strong and true. He'll be protected and loved by all the dragons of my land. I can assure you of that. And he'll be respected as he grows. Ice Dragons are not to be trifled with and he'll grow into that responsibility with our guidance."

Roland pulled her close and kissed her long and hard, his hot tongue sweeping into her mouth and lighting a fire in her belly she'd never felt before. His strong hands swept up her smooth legs, rubbing beneath the hem of her tunic and up the curves of her ass as she struggled mindlessly to get closer to him. She'd never felt such passion, such heady delight.

His warm palm spread over the curve of her rear, shocking a gasp from her lips that he swallowed as he took her to the ground once more. His hard body pressed along her length, his hand roaming as he dragged the hem of her tunic upwards. His fingers searched for and found the heavy curve of her breast, making her shiver. When he palmed her nipple, she couldn't suppress the moan of pleasure that sounded from her throat, but when he closed his thumb and forefinger around her hard peak and tugged, she nearly screamed.

Only his heavy weight above her kept her on the ground, so violent was the urge to move as her insides fired hot and heavy. He pulled back from her lips to stare down into her eyes. Flames leapt within his dark green gaze as he continued tugging rhythmically on her nipple.

"I want you, Lana. I want to make love with you, be inside you, shoot my seed deep within your womb and mark you as mine." His hands caressed her flaming hair as the dragon within him roared to life possessively. "You're mine, Lana. Mine!" He paused to take a deep breath, regaining some control. "Never doubt that. I knew almost from the first that you were made for me."

"Roland—"

She wanted to protest but he cut off her words by kissing her again. His hand moved on her breast and liquid fire raced through her veins, not to be outdone by a strange, wet sensation between her legs. She didn't know what was happening to her. Roland moved his other hand to explore the moisture and she felt her cheeks heat with embarrassment, but his expression grew impossibly hotter as he pulled back to smile down at her.

"You're so wet for me."

"I'm sorry—"

"Oh, baby, don't be embarrassed. That's what's supposed to happen when a woman prepares to take a man inside her body. Without that miracle wetness, we wouldn't fit together comfortably. Your body's response tells me you want me." He moved one finger inside her. She gasped at the fullness and new sensations bombarding her. It felt so good.

Then he did something with his thumb, moving it around a little nubbin of flesh that sent her shooting straight up to the stars. She sobbed softly as she trembled against him, her gaze seeking his for reassurance. He smiled down at her, his fingers stroking and petting, his eyes hot but somehow kind as he watched her reach a peak she hadn't even known was there.

"Roland!" Her breathless whisper sparked desire in his gaze as he slowly removed his hand from between her legs. With a devilish smile, he brought his wet fingers to his lips and licked them clean.

"You taste divine, Lana. Now do you understand better what I meant when I said I wanted to eat you yesterday?" She felt the flush rise up her cheeks thinking about what those shocking words implied. His mouth dove for her neck, sighing and sucking on her delicate skin as he teased her. "I want to lick your pussy and have you come against my tongue. I want all of you, Lana. Will you give yourself to me?"

She didn't know what she would have answered because at that moment, both of them heard Tor shifting not too far away. The dragonet was stirring and would soon wake.

Roland pulled away to look deep into her eyes. "Will you keep this one secret for me? It won't be for long. Just for a while. All the dragons in my land know the truth, except the children."

She looked over at her baby, Tor, and realized this was not something that would harm him. She nodded her agreement.

"I won't tell him. It's your secret to share, Roland."

He swooped down to kiss her once more and then pulled back, a look of regret on his face. He held her gaze with his own for as long as possible while a magical black swirl of mist formed around his body. He grew and lengthened, his face becoming that of the dragon while his arm transformed once again into his sheltering wing. His body thickened and within moments the black dragon was back beside her, holding her close to his warm side.

"That is just amazing."

Thank you. I'm glad I could finally impress you.

"So why didn't you change before now? Were you too badly wounded?"

Exactly so. Between your healing sessions and our reciprocal energy sharing while we sleep, I healed well enough that this morning was the first time I could shift without fear. Wounds that are mere scratches to me in this form would kill me if I wore my human form.

"Amazing. What do you mean about sharing energy while we sleep?"

Caught that, did you? His dark eyes sparkled down at her in the gray morning light. *It's a phenomenon I've never experienced before, but I've read about it in the ancient texts. You gave your healing to me while I slept, but somehow we managed to connect in our unconscious, and neither of us was drained. You received the energy from me, and then directed it back as waves of healing energy, changed by your touch. It's a partnership of sorts, a deep bond that we share.*

"I didn't even realize." Her thoughts sped to keep up with the ideas he was laying out before her.

I know. I didn't at first either, but I felt the healing, even while we slept, then I remembered the teachings of my youth about the legends of the royal line and the remarkable females who had amazing gifts of healing. That's why I have no doubts about who you are, Lana. Your special power speaks to me.

She settled back against his side, liking his words, as she mulled over all that had happened since Tor had helped him back to their cold, little lair in the mountains.

"You saw me naked!" Her outrage was ruined by the little giggle that left her lips as she smacked his side gently. "I thought you were a dragon, but all the while I let you look at me and you were human too." She blushed remembering his warm breath drying her bare body and the way his faceted emerald gaze had followed her. "I should have known."

He let out a smoky chuckle. *Yes, you should have realized by the way my tongue was practically hanging out of my mouth. You are one gorgeous woman, Lana. I mean that sincerely. How could I resist looking at such beauty when presented so enticingly before me?*

Lana! Are you awake? Tor's happy voice spoke to both minds.

"Yes, I'm awake, Tor." She raised her voice so the dragonet could hear her. "How are you this morning?"

I'm good. I want to fly.

Me too, Roland added in a dry voice, stretching his wings as he made a show of waking up. Tor followed suit, getting up and bounding over to one of the larger pools to play at fishing for a few minutes.

Shall we gather your things and get underway? The sun is high enough now to really sparkle off Tor's magnificent scales. Roland was speaking to her alone, she knew. She answered him in the silence of their minds to keep their words private between just the two of them.

You really were serious about that?

Roland snorted smokily as she got up and stretched. His gaze followed her with a hungry glitter.

Dragons can be just as impressed by the look of their fellows as humans. Believe me, Tor is going to make quite an impression when my friends get a good look at him, and I do have an ulterior motive. If they're looking at him, the knights won't be making eyes at you. His large head butted into her soft breasts gently. *I might not be able to keep from toasting a few of them if they start making a play for my girl.*

Is that what I am? Your girl?

Roland stood very still, watching her closely. *I'd like that, Lana, and more. I'll make no secret of how I feel. We belong together.*

This is all happening so fast.

I know. I've had a few days to think about it. You only just found out I can shift from dragon to man. It's a lot to take in and I know I'm rushing things but you can't deny that we feel right together, can you?

She took a moment before answering him honestly, in a small voice. *No, I can't deny it.*

Then I won't press you for an answer now, but think about it, Lana. I want you.

Chapter Five

Roland led them over the river only a few minutes later, and within moments, a trumpeting call challenged them from above. Two dragons and knights bore down on them, flanking their flight as soon as they saw Roland's black hide. She guessed the other dragons and their riders must be talking silently with Roland, but none made any attempt to speak with either her or Tor from what she could tell.

Look at them, Lana! They're such pretty colors. Tor's voice was admiring as he looked at the other dragons—the first he had ever seen besides Roland.

Yes, they are pretty, sweetheart, but none are as shiny and sparkly as you.

She noted the looks Tor's shining scales garnered from both the dragons and the knights on their backs as they winged toward the Lair Roland had told them about. There was a lovely golden dragon and a shiny, coppery red one, both just a bit smaller than Tor but larger than Roland in size.

Roland's last words were still ringing through her mind, tingling through her body. He'd said he wanted her and the deep growl in his words stirred her womb to life. She'd tasted her first passion just that morning, under his gentle hands, and she wanted more. Oh, how she wanted more of that sweet pleasure! But she was afraid too. As a slave in Salomar's house, she'd seen the worst of men and their dishonor.

While she doubted Roland was anything like any of the swine she'd evaded in Salomar's realm, he was still male, and therefore a largely unknown quantity to her. He was also—startlingly—a dragon too. She didn't know what to make of his dual nature. She knew only one dragon, and Tor was just a baby. She remembered vague tales of knights and dragons from her youth, but never had she heard about men who became dragons and vice versa.

The magic swirling around Roland frightened her just a bit. His aggressive passion tantalized her, and the fire in his eyes warmed her very bones. He'd said he wanted her, and Mother help her, she realized she wanted him too. The only question was when—not if. She'd never been more certain of anything in her life. She wanted to know the fullness of Roland's passion. Where it would lead them, only the Mother of All knew for sure. Lana would do her best to take one step at a time. For now, she would follow where he led to meet his people and the dragons of the Northern Lair.

When what she assumed was the landing ledge of the Lair was in sight, both the dragons and knights who escorted them veered off, allowing Roland to land first, followed by Tor and Lana. Immediately, the respect of the other dragons and knights in the area was obvious. They made way for Roland, bowing their heads respectfully, though they didn't lower their eyes. She liked that. She liked how they showed respect but maintained their own dignity, unlike the way Salomar had demanded people bow and scrape before him.

Lana climbed down from Tor's back and unwrapped the head covering that she used to keep warm at altitude. She heard a few gasps as her long auburn hair was revealed and intercepted a few shocked looks from knights who couldn't seem to help staring at her and Tor. She kept close to Tor's side as they followed in Roland's steps. He seemed to know where he was going, so she let him lead, craning her neck to see all she could of the strange tunnels and caves that had been ornately carved into the living rock.

The Lair was clean and warm, filled with dozens of dragons and their knights. Few women were about, but everyone looked clean and well-kept. The knights were all big men, bulging with muscle, and they had the look of hardened warriors. The dragons were colorful, sleek and strong, though mostly smaller than Tor, but only by a little. Of course, Tor was still a growing boy.

Roland turned in at a large central chamber, announcing himself with a short blast of sound that was sort of a rumbling cough. She followed with Tor and immediately saw two dragons raise their heads out of a deep oval pit filled with sand. One was green and one a sort of blue color that was almost green. They were obviously a mated pair, for a moment later she saw a smaller dragon who was also greenish in hue and looked a lot like her parents.

Roland spoke first, including them all in his thoughts.

Greetings Tilden, Rue and little Rena. I've brought some new friends for you to meet.

The green dragon raised his head to look over at Tor.

Any friend of yours, sire, is welcome in our home.

Thank you, old friend. May I introduce you to Tor? Despite his size, he's about the same age as Rena and I thought perhaps they could play together under your guidance while I seek out your knights and their mate.

The bluish female dragon nodded, looking over at Tor with obvious surprise. *You are big for your age, aren't you?*

Roland thinks I'm an Ice Dragon. Tor was so sweet and innocent, his guileless words made the older dragons snort with amusement.

No doubt you are, my lad, the green climbed nimbly out of the pit and walked over to Tor. *I've never seen such pure crystal scales on any of my brethren in this land, though I did once catch sight of an Ice Dragon when I was just a youngster on a mission to the far north. I'll never forget the sight, so sparkling and bright. Just like you.*

Tor bowed his head bashfully.

Tor's never met any other dragons. Besides Roland, I mean. Lana couldn't help her protective thoughts from escaping though she hadn't been properly introduced to the strange dragon who stood so near. Both of the strange dragons turned to watch her in surprise. *Please be kind to him. He's still so young and he doesn't know your ways.*

You are bonded to him? It was the female dragon who spoke, her words thick with incredulity.

The tone raised every protective instinct Lana had. She stepped in front of Tor, facing down the two adult dragons. *We look out for each other.*

Amazing. The green dragon dipped his head closer to inspect her. Lana refused to back down or be intimidated. Tor would defend her, she knew, and she would defend him to her dying breath if need be.

It was the little greenish dragonet who broke the tense silence. Kicking up sand with her wings as she struggled out of the deep pit, she moved over to Tor and butted her head against his long neck.

Are you really my age? You're so big!

Lana says I'm five winters old. How old are you?

The smaller dragon ducked her head shyly. *Only four winters. Will you play with me though? The others say I'm too little.*

Tor gave a smoky chuckle and moved his head under hers, tapping lightly. *Everybody here seems little to me, but you're nice. I'll play with you.*

I think we have an accord, Roland said dryly, chuckling as they all watched the two dragonets with loving indulgence. He turned his

67

attention back to the adults, speaking to them and Lana privately. *If you would be so kind as to watch them closely. Lana is right. Tor has never met any other dragons. She's cared for him since before he hatched and is the only friend he's ever known.*

You've mother-bonded with him! The female dragon couldn't seem to hold back her amazement.

I don't know what that is, but we love each other and have been together every day since he was born.

Forgive me. Roland tilted his head. *Lana, this is Tilden and Rue. They and their knights are the elders of this Lair. Tor will be in good hands with them.*

Lana looked back at Tor with uncertain eyes.

We'll look after him as if he were our own, the green dragon assured her with a grave bow of his head. *Any request from Roland is one we are happy to fulfill. Besides, Rena has been lonely. There are no dragonets her age here and the older ones pick on her a bit more than I like. Having a big, strong friend might be good for her, if you get my meaning.* The green blinked one of his emerald eyes slyly and Lana had to chuckle at the picture he made.

I understand. Thank you for agreeing to look after him. She bowed her head, keeping her eyes up as she had seen the others in this strange Lair do and was rewarded with a similar show of respect from Tilden.

Excellent. Roland called their attention back to more immediate matters. *Now, would you be so kind as to ask your knights and their mate to meet us here while you take the children out for a bit so we can get down to business? There is grave news from the north.*

As we feared. Rue ducked her bluish head. *We will listen through our knights while we watch the littles.*

The news is not good, but there is hope yet for all of us, and he's standing behind me. If they fly, watch him carefully. He's got moves even I can't match.

We're going to need to learn them if we are to outsmart the weapons Salomar has been devising.

"Weapons?"

A gruff male voice sounded from the large doorway. Lana guessed it had to be one of the knights. No doubt the adult dragons had opened a link to their bonded knights the moment Roland requested their presence.

The knight was tall, broad shouldered and brown haired, a warrior through and through. Lana found herself backing away toward Tor and Roland as the strange man was joined by an equally large, blond warrior and long-limbed woman who had kind, but shrewd blue eyes.

Wait 'til the children are gone, Hal, please. Roland's voice seemed amusedly exasperated.

The warrior called Hal walked up to little Rena and stroked her back as he passed, eyeing Tor with confusion. "Don't tell me he's not full grown yet."

He's not. Roland included all of them in his thoughts, making the introductions. *Tor, Lana, this is Hal. The blonde knight is Jures and the lady is their mate, Candis.*

I'm five. Tor dipped his head, and the adults were obviously touched and amused by his candor.

Lana wondered at the introduction but didn't know how to ask outright about the woman being mate to both knights. If this really was the land of her birth, she didn't remember three-partnered marriages being the norm, and while Salomar was a pig, a few of the servants she'd known were married and they only had one mate each. Still, it would be worse than rude to question these people who were obviously highly ranked and friends of Roland's. She made a mental note to ask him later, if she got a chance.

Roland forestalled the conjecture about Tor by shooing the dragonets out with his thick, black wings. The older dragons followed behind with amused glances at the surprised humans they left behind in the doorway. As soon as they were gone, Roland transformed, calling up the black mist, clouding his change from dragon to human form.

"That's better," he said when he was human once more, clothed in fine black leathers. Lana drank in the sight of him. He was so handsome, it hurt. "Lana, my dear," he took her hands. He led her to another room in the suite that had couches and chairs, seating her close at his side on the couch, practically in his lap. The others followed with bemused looks on their faces.

"We expected you days ago, sire. What kept you?" It was the blonde warrior who spoke as he poured out several glasses of wine from a table at the side of the room.

"Salomar has nasty giant crossbows with diamond-bladed bolts. I got hit with three of them before Tor and Lana came to my rescue." Gasps sounded from all around. Moments later, three pairs of curious eyes settled on Lana, going between her and Roland, eager for answers.

Roland sighed. "It was my own stupid fault. I assumed nothing could pierce my hide. Boy, was I wrong."

"You were hurt badly?" the woman, Candis, asked with concern.

"I thought I was dead. I would have been too, if not for Tor and Lana. Tor is amazingly strong and was able to tow me back to their lair. Lana is a dragon healer."

Stunned silence greeted that statement until finally Hal spoke. "Lucky is too inadequate a word to describe you, Rol. The Mother was watching your path for certain." The brown-haired knight shook his head as he raised his glass in silent toast.

"I don't doubt it, my friend." Roland squeezed Lana's hand, which he still held. "I think Lana is one of the twin daughters of Adora of Kent for whom we've been searching. I'm leaving with her and Tor tomorrow for the palace. I want one of your messengers to get word to Adora and her daughter, Belora. I want them both to come to the palace as soon as possible. It's about time we all met, and if I'm right, it will be a joyous reunion."

"We'll send a messenger right away," Hal affirmed with a nod.

"Good. Now to less pleasant matters. Salomar is almost certainly allied with Skithdron and planning attacks across this border with weapons designed to take down dragons. Lana," he turned to her, "you've seen them and fought them. How would you describe the different weapons Salomar brought against you and Tor?"

"Well, there are the big crossbows that hit you, and then he's got some catapult things that throw big chunks of sharp stuff that can slice through dragon scale. Tor got hit with that just once and he was bleeding from about a dozen cuts. We got out of there fast and learned how to avoid them as much as possible. Salomar has also used his witch against us several times. She has this way of slipping into Tor's mind and making him do what she wants. I didn't even notice it at first. She's very subtle. But when I realized we were heading for a trap I was able to cut her connection with Tor, pull him back through our link and turn him away from the warriors waiting to take him down."

"I've never heard of such a thing." Hal's eyes narrowed in thought. "Are you certain about this witch? Few females can even talk to dragons, much less influence one to that degree. Maybe it's because he's so young?"

Lana shook her head. "I saw her make Tor's mother forget all about her egg and fly away without a second look. It's not because he's young."

"That's criminal! Deliberately separating a mother and her baby." Candis looked truly outraged and it warmed Lana's heart.

"Tell us how you came to care for Tor." Roland's soft voice took her out of her anger and back to the past.

"I was a slave in Salomar's household. He threw me in with the egg and barred the exit so neither of us could get out. I was to keep the fires lit so the egg stayed warm. After a while, I realized by accident that I could talk with the baby inside if I touched the shell. After he grew more, we could talk even when I wasn't touching the shell. Then he hatched." Her eyes misted in memory. "Salomar thought I would be his first meal but Tor ate the dogs he loosed on me instead. From that moment to this, he's protected me every bit and more than I've looked after him. When he got big enough and could fly, we escaped and have been running and hiding ever since."

"You are a brave and noble woman, milady." Hal bowed his head to her, his eyes solemn as the others followed suit. She was overwhelmed by their show of respect and unable to answer such compliments.

Roland hugged her close, tucking her blushing cheek against his chest. "I agree," he said softly, though all of them heard his words. "You're a treasure, Lana. You saved my life."

She moved back a bit to look up at him. "Don't forget Tor."

Roland chuckled. "How could I forget Tor? He's a miracle, as are you—the only woman ever known to tame a wild northern Ice Dragon. Bards will sing of you for generations to come, I'm sure."

They all laughed at his grand statement and Lana was back to blushing, but the mood was considerably lighter. They talked for a few more minutes about plans for the rest of their stay in the Northern Lair and preparations they could make to defend against the new weapons that might be brought against them all. Finally though, the agenda was set and Lana could tell Roland was in a bit of pain from his still-healing wounds.

"Lady Candis, do you think you could find something for Lana to wear?" Roland stood and all the rest followed suit. "I'd like to show her around the Lair a bit and I promised her a stop at the baths."

"I think we can come up with something that will work for the time being." The other woman smiled in her friendly way and stood, motioning for Lana to join her. "Come with me, my dear, and we'll see what we can find in my closet."

Lana went with the other woman, comforted by her easy manner. The dragons were still out of the suite and she looked curiously at the big, empty oval of sand as they skirted it on their way to another of the many rooms arranged around the sand pit.

"I've never seen so much sand in one place before," Lana commented.

Lady Candis appeared surprised but smiled warmly. "The dragons love it. The fine grains polish their hides and the warmth appeals to them, of course. Our rooms are built around their wallow and as you can see, the arches are wide enough that they can lay their heads in the doors of most of our rooms, so we can all be together almost anywhere in this suite."

"It's ingenious." A moment later, they entered a big room with a huge bed at its center. The walls were hung with rich fabrics so colorful they brought tears to her eyes. "Oh, this room is beautiful!" Lana's words were heartfelt as her eyes absorbed the lovely mix of colors and textures.

"Thank you," Candis said quietly, watching Lana with interest. Lana knew her reactions must seem strange to the other woman, but she just couldn't help herself.

"It's just that…" Lana tried to find the right words to express herself. "I've been on the run for a long time, living in the wild with Tor. I remember a little from the time before, when I lived with my mother and sisters, but it's been so long, and we never had such fine things." Her voice trailed off as her emotions threatened to overwhelm her. Candis surprised her by placing a sisterly arm around her shoulders, hugging her comfortingly.

"Come on, Lana. Let's find something gorgeous for you to wear." She pulled her toward the large closet along one wall. "I bet I have just the thing to bring out your beautiful eyes and impress the heck out of Roland."

Lana felt her cheeks heat with a blush. "He's seen me at my worst already, Lady Candis. I doubt anything could change his opinion of me. Besides, he's much too grand for the likes of me."

"Nonsense!" Candis swept a shining green dress out of the closet, splashing the full skirt across the bed. Lana caught her breath at its beauty. "He's smitten with you already. I can tell. This will finish the job, and luckily it's cut well enough that it will fit you properly, even though you're a bit shorter than me."

"Oh! I couldn't wear that." Lana backed away from the temptation of the gorgeous satin dress.

Candis picked it up and draped it against Lana's shoulders. "Of course you can. What's more, it's yours now. A welcome gift from me to you. I hope you wear it in happiness."

Lana held out her hands to gently fend her off, but Candis draped the dress over her arms, not taking no for an answer. Lana protested a bit more, but Candis eventually got her way, ushering Lana out of the chamber, the new owner of a lovely, green satin dress.

Before she knew it, Lana was walking beside Roland through the corridors of the Northern Lair. The few people they passed bowed slightly as they passed, making her feel a bit self-conscious, but there was real respect in the people's eyes, not just formal obedience, which impressed her. She realized Roland was royalty, probably a prince, though he hadn't told her exactly what place he held in the kingdom and she was too flustered to ask.

They made their way to the landing ledge and Lana found herself scanning the skies for any sign of Tor. There were so many dragons! It was a breathtaking sight to see. Tears came to her eyes as she spotted Tor frolicking through the air, his scales glistening brighter than any other. He was playing a game of tag with his little friend Rena, slowing his flight, she knew, to allow the littler baby dragon to catch him up. She saw the cliffs all around were dotted with perched dragons, all eyes watching the Ice Dragonet in their midst.

"Why are they all watching him like that?"

Roland put a reassuring arm around her shoulders.

"They're fascinated by him, I think. Ice Dragons are the stuff of legend, even here. Plus, they're watching his flight patterns. He's the first wild dragon we've seen in my lifetime. Maybe longer than that. All of them," he pointed to indicate the scores of dragons watching from the cliffs, "were trained to fly the same way. Just as I was. We all know the same tricks and the same flight patterns. Tor presents a unique chance to see how a wild dragon flies. I can attest to the fact that he has tricks none of us have ever even considered trying. We can learn a lot from him, especially how he manages to evade Salomar's new weapons."

She liked the respect she heard in Roland's voice. "He'll be happy, I'm sure, to show you what he knows. He was hurt many times by those weapons before he figured out what to do to avoid them. He has a good heart, Roland, and he won't want to see any other dragons injured, captured, or even killed by Salomar and his men."

"I was hoping that would be the case." He turned her in his arms, catching and holding her gaze. "I meant what I said. You and Tor have a new home here in Draconia, with me. Not just because we can learn from you, but because you belong here, Lana. Both of you need to be with others of your kind. Tor needs other dragons and you need to reunite with your family." He pulled her in for a quick kiss. "And I need you, Lana. I need you in my life."

"Oh, Roland." He cut off what she would have said with his kiss, deep and lingering, and hot. She felt his desire, though she'd never experienced a man's ardor before meeting Roland.

At length he drew back and Lana finally noticed the grins aimed at them from other knights in the area. She blushed to the roots of her fiery hair as Roland chuckled, hugging her close.

"Come on." He turned her, keeping one strong arm around her shoulders as he walked them away from the ledge. "Now you've seen for yourself that Tor's fine, how about the bath I promised you?"

Chapter Six

Roland grabbed some clean towels, scented soaps and lotions from the anteroom right in front of the main entrance to the Lair's communal baths. He had a hard time hiding his desire, but Lana was so innocent, she barely noticed the evidence of his fierce arousal. Sweet Mother, how she set him aflame!

She was like no other woman he had ever known, and he'd known more than his share of beauties. All those other women meant nothing to him since meeting Lana. She was the only woman in the world who mattered. Her soft smile, her gentle voice, her undying loyalty to the dragonet—all those things made him admire her and want her in his life. Her unvarnished beauty and exciting, healing touch also made him want her in his bed.

"The air is so moist and heavy." Her green eyes were wide as she went forward with him, cautiously, into the large cavern.

"The pools here are heated by the earth beneath. The waters are full of minerals that are good for your health and kind to the skin." He guided her into the main chamber, pointing to the various pools and amenities. "There's one large pool for swimming and play. It's not quite as hot as the bathing pools, but still therapeutic for strained muscles and good for exercise." He pointed to the largest, closest of the pools and she was shocked to see a few men there, swimming naked through the water.

"Are those men knights?"

He saw her wide, innocent eyes glued to one man's ass as he cut his way through the water and Roland realized with an inner growl that he didn't want her looking at other men. Only him. The dragon inside him reared up in defiance. She was his. Didn't she know that?

Roland pulled her around to face him as gently as he could manage, but he could tell he'd startled her. At times it was hard to reconcile his dragon instincts with his human side. He took a deep breath to try to calm himself before speaking.

"The only man you need be interested in is before you, Lana." He held her firmly, reading confusion in her eyes that made him feel like a jealous idiot. He released her, lifting each finger individually off her arm. It was that difficult for him to get control of his more primitive emotions.

"To answer your question, all the men in this Lair are either knights or the sons of knights. The youngsters tend to various tasks in the Lair as they get older, and many are chosen by dragons if they're good, honorable lads, when their time comes. Those who aren't chosen as knights often find service with the army or the royal guard."

"Are they all warriors then?"

He was glad to see she seemed merely curious. "No, not all, but most. All children who grow up in a Lair study the fighting arts to some degree. Many choose to follow the path of the warrior even if they aren't chosen as knights. There are notable exceptions, of course. My friend Drake is the son of a knight and also a highly regarded bard. Drake left his family and Lair at a young age to study abroad. My brother sees him often in his travels and teases Drake that if he'd stayed in Draconia, he'd no doubt be a knight by now. But Drake just shakes his head and laughs. Still, I think there's more to him than just clever tales and rhyme. And I know the dragons think so too. But he's stubborn."

Roland shrugged, dismissing the thoughts of his friend and motioned Lana forward again. He steered her gently toward the carved half-wall separating the main pool from several others at the rear of the huge chamber. He stopped in front of a dimly lit, more private pool, smaller than the others, with bubbles rising clearly on the surface of the faintly metallic-smelling water.

"This pool is one of my favorites. It's a bit hotter than the others, but the water is effervescent and very relaxing." It was his dragon nature that enjoyed the higher temperatures, and he'd bet Lana would enjoy it as well, being half-dragon herself.

He watched her carefully as she stepped to the rim, bending to run her hand through the water. Smiling, her eyes lit with pleasure and he knew he'd been right. She couldn't be a more perfect match for him—even in this small, seemingly insignificant way.

"The bubbles tickle! And it's so warm."

Lana stood, turning to him. She gasped when she saw he was already naked. Roland draped the towels he'd brought over a handy bench and stepped forward to take Lana's hand. She was frightened, he could tell by the slight tremble of her fingers, but so far curiosity seemed to be outweighing fear. Her gaze tracked over him from head to toe, lingering in the middle, on the proof of his desire pointing, hard and ready, at the woman it most wanted in all the world.

"You know," Roland stalked forward, "being half-dragon makes me a bit different from most men, but then," his hands moved gently to the lacings of her top, "you're half-dragon as well." He slowly untied

79

the lacings on her clothes, tugging gently as he bared her luscious skin inch by inch. Her eyes widened and fire flared in their depths, but she raised no objection. The dragon in him rumbled in pleasure. "It should be interesting for both of us, being with our own kind. I bet," he bared her breasts with one smooth move, allowing her top to fall away down over her smooth shoulders, "neither of us will have to hold back with the other. We can share all that we are, with no fear. It will be a novel experience."

"I don't want to be just a novelty to you, Roland." Lana's spine straightened as he pushed her pants down those lovely, long legs, but she didn't stop him. He felt the hunger grow sharper as he rose, facing her once more.

Roland stilled, cupping her neck in one broad palm and drawing her forward as their gazes locked and held. His lips traced over hers lightly, in a gentle salute, before he drew back to rest his forehead against hers.

"I keep forgetting how innocent you are. Forgive me, sweetheart." Roland sighed and his warm breath stirred her hair. "The beast inside me wants to trumpet to the heavens, drag you to my lair and spend the rest of my days making love to you." He felt her shiver and she surprised him by leaning up to place a tiny kiss on the side of his mouth.

"Then why don't you?" Kicking off her shoes, she stepped out of the pants that had pooled around her ankles, flinging them away with one foot as she lingered within his embrace.

"Right now you don't need the beast, Lana. You need the man. I don't want to hurt you or scare you. I want you to feel safe with me."

She moved even closer, wrapping her hands around his neck. She laid her cheek in the hollow of his shoulder, snuggling into him like a warm kitten. He reveled in the heat of her that nearly matched his own. He'd had his share of women since he was a young lad, but never had he found one so perfectly matched to him. Never had a woman felt so right, nor been so unafraid of his fire. Roland's body temperature rose as the dragon prowled in his soul, but she just cuddled closer, completely unafraid of his fire.

"You've kept me safe 'til now. I've never trusted anyone the way I trust you, Roland."

He cupped her curvy ass in his broad hands, holding her close for long moments. Splashing sounds from the other side of the wall reminded him they were not alone in the large chamber, though their private tub was well out of the line of sight of the main area. Still, others could walk back here easily enough to use one of the nearby pools. Though none would intrude on their pool unless invited—he was royalty after all—they would feel free using the other smaller pools nearby, he knew. A few of the men would probably come back here just to get a better look at Lana. Women who could live among dragons were rare and rumors were probably already flying about Lana and the remarkable entrance she'd made with Tor.

"Let's get in the water."

He squeezed her once before lifting her high in his arms. She was light as a feather, her skin warm and supple, and her eyes glowed with fire and fun as he looked down at her. He had to stop a moment and kiss her. He couldn't wait to feel her lips under his.

With a rumbling groan, he plundered her mouth, turning her in his embrace as he paused just at the edge of the small pool. Her warm skin tantalized him, her responsive mouth drugged him. Only the sounds of male voices and more splashing from the other side of the cavern roused him. For himself, Roland didn't care who witnessed him taking his woman, but he knew she was inexperienced and probably a little shy. He didn't want to shock her too much their first time out, but there would come a time…oh yes, indeed, there would be time for them to let loose and indulge all their desires.

Tugging his mouth away, even as she tried to follow and bring him back to her kiss, Roland stepped down the carved ledge into the bubbling water. He moved slowly, dipping her into the water step by step, letting her acclimate to the temperature. It was hotter than most human women would enjoy, he knew, but he reveled in the knowledge she was like him, half-dragon within her soul. Because of that and the way she'd been forced to live to this point, she was totally out of his realm of experience when it came to women.

He liked that. He liked the idea that she was as new to him as he was to her. For once, a relationship with a female would start off on even footing. If he had the true measure of Lana, it would remain so, and oddly, he liked that idea even more. They were superbly matched. He felt like growling in triumph, but tamped his innate aggression down as much as he could manage.

"Is it too hot?" he asked, concern for her put above his desire.

She lowered her legs as he released them. "No, it's lovely. So warm and bubbly. I like it."

He saw the fire leap in her eyes as the water burst in bubbles against her delicate skin. She was a sensuous marvel to him, so innocent, yet so wanton. He showed her briefly how to use the scrubbing sand he'd brought to gently rub her soft skin and indulged himself in the pleasant task of soaping up her beautiful auburn hair. His fingers sunk deep into her tresses and massaged her scalp, her back to his front as she let him touch her, closing her eyes and making sultry, little sounds of pleasure in the back of her throat as he worked.

"Roland?" Her voice sounded hesitant and he paused slightly, fighting to keep his erection away from her for just a little longer. He didn't want to scare her off.

"Yes, sweetling?"

"Can I ask you a question?"

He paused to kiss her shoulder. "You can ask me anything you want at any time. I'll do my best to answer, though I don't promise to know everything."

"It's about, um, your friends Candis, Jures and Hal. Um."

He peeked over her shoulder amused by the way she was biting the corner of one luscious lip. He fought the fierce desire to turn her and nibble on her lips himself.

"Well, I was wondering how that works. One woman and two men. Are they married like my parents were? Is it a permanent thing? And why do they do it? I noticed several other trios in the halls as we walked. Is that normal here?"

Her voice was pitched low but he clearly heard the curiosity and the slight catch in her words. Perhaps she was a bit more than curious. Intrigued, might be a good word, he thought, as the dragon in him roared to life. He had to fight against half his nature to keep his calm and answer her innocent question.

"Yes, it's normal for knights of mated dragons to share a wife between them. Because the knights bond deeply and permanently with their dragon partners, when the dragons mate, the knights are often overcome by the mating frenzy. It's the reason dragons are forbidden to mate unless their knight partner also has a mate. Without a mate to love and share their passion, the knight would soon run mad, and just a casual sex partner won't suffice. There must be the depth of emotion— love and passion—to sate the frenzy. Just as it is for the dragons."

"But dragons only have one mate, right?"

He couldn't help it. His arms tightened around her reflexively, bringing her back in close to his chest, her sweet round ass against his hardness. She gasped and stiffened only for a moment, then relaxed into him, soothing his volatile temper.

"We dragons mate for life. One mate only. So you'll never have to even think about being shared between two knights, Lana. You are mine alone."

She gasped and pulled away, turning to face him. "That sounds pretty serious, Roland."

He stalked toward her. "I am serious. I told you before. I want you in my life. I'm no knight to share my woman with another husband. I'm a dragon and I want you all to myself, so you can just forget any ideas you had about any other man right now."

She laughed, stilling him instantly. Why in the world did she find him funny?

"Oh, Roland, I don't want another man." She blushed furiously, enchanting him. "I was just curious about your people and how they live. Candis seems happy with her mates but I don't think I could do that."

He closed the remaining distance between them and pulled her into his arms loosely, sighing. He had to get control of his temper, lest he frighten her off.

"You won't ever have to do anything you don't want to do, Lana. The Mother of All guides the knights and dragons in their choice of mates. I doubt She will be guiding any knight or dragon to you." He kissed her sweetly then pulled back and held her gaze as he brought his hard body against her lower half. She gasped. "I found you first."

He kissed her deeply then, squeezing her close, aligning their bodies and stroking his hips against hers. He slid his hard rod between her thighs, teasing her folds but taking it no further. He'd be damned if he would take her virginity in such a public place.

Still, he could show her a bit of what she was in for later that night. He wouldn't wait longer than that to make her completely his.

Roland moved back near the edge of the pool. Indentations had been cut into the rock at different levels, leaving convenient little ledges below the water so people could sit and relax. He led her to the highest of them still beneath the water and sat her down, facing him. Holding her gaze, he swept one large hand down to settle between her legs, spreading her gently as he coaxed her with his fingers and encouraged her with his smile.

"Let me give you pleasure, little one. Let me give you joy." He moved close and claimed her lips and she melted against him, squirming closer as he insinuated his fingers into her virgin tightness.

The ledge he had her on was about a foot deep in the water. Her beautiful breasts bobbed above the surface, tempting him. With a harsh groan, he moved his head down to lick the tender globes, stroking his tongue downward to circle around the taut nipple as she gasped.

He sucked her nipple in deep, teasing gently with his teeth as he allowed one long finger to slide inside her tight warmth. She squirmed as he prepared her for what would come later that night. She was virgin, but she was willing—more than willing, in fact, if her half-wild responses were anything to go by. He would savor the moments to come when he breached her for the first time. He would take her again and again, and right now he wasn't quite sure if he would ever be able to take his fill from her.

He moved to her other breast, sucking her deep and expertly flicking his tongue, all the while plying her clit with his fingers, until he knew she was on the very precipice, ready to tumble over. Her little body was shaking with need as he eased up from her breasts, seeking her gaze.

But she wasn't looking at him. Her wide green eyes were focused on something over his shoulder. Curious, he turned to find several of the knights watching them from a small pool just a few yards away. Growling, he saw her effect on them. Half of them were already stroking their cocks under the water, watching his woman near her climax. At least they knew enough not to come too near him when he was in this state. A dragon interrupted in the middle of pleasure was a dangerous animal indeed.

The knights kept a respectful distance from him, but their eyes followed Lana's supple movements as she writhed in his arms. That she wasn't screaming bloody murder surprised him. She was shocked, he could tell by her wide eyes, but whether she was shocked at the knights watching or at her own response to their lustful eyes on her bare body, he wasn't sure.

When dragons mated, it was out in the open and most dragons had an exhibitionist streak in their nature. Perhaps the dragon part of her soul was shining through, Roland mused as Lana whimpered and moaned, nearing ecstasy from his touch.

"Do you like that?" he growled next to her ear, pitching his voice so only she could hear as he stroked lightly in and out of her delicate channel with his finger. "Do you like knowing that they're watching you? Fantasizing about being the one sliding into your warm heat? Giving you pleasure?"

She moaned softly as he increased his pace. Looking up, he caught her eyes. "They can look, but none of them will ever touch you, my Lana. Only me."

Driven, he moved swiftly, lifting her out of the water and positioning her on the smooth stone ledge to his satisfaction. She gasped as he spread her legs and settled his head between them, licking her from anus to clit with his exceptionally hot tongue.

"Come up on your elbows, sweetling," he ordered. When she met his gaze, down in the V of her spread legs, she blushed deep and hot. He liked that. "Now look at them, Lana. Watch them watching you. Watching us. Tug on your nipples for me."

She did as he ordered, moving her eyes up to the men across the way. They were all stroking their cocks aggressively now, he saw out of the corner of his eye. He focused on her as her limbs trembled, her fire spiking higher as he sucked her little clit, moving his finger back to tease her pussy and adding a slight pressure with his thumb on the tight rosette of her ass. She gasped as her gaze jumped back to his.

"Watch them, Lana. Let them see your pleasure."

He pushed in with both fingers while sucking gently on her clit. He rubbed his agile tongue over her most sensitive part, sending her to the stars with pleasure that shot through her trembling body. She spasmed against him, moaning, then giving him little panting cries that fired his blood. He heard groans from a few yards distant and knew the knights were finding their own completion as they watched him pleasure his woman. They were single men with little hope of finding a compatible mate anytime soon, so he didn't begrudge them this small glimpse of their passion. Still, if any one of them even thought of touching his woman, he'd fry them where they stood.

The lines were clear. He was a black dragon and this was his woman. None of them would cross that line. The code of honor among knights and dragons was too strong to allow otherwise.

With a triumphant grin, he swept Lana into his arms as she spiraled down from the peak she'd discovered at his hands. He felt good knowing his woman was so responsive to his touch and even a little more daring than he would have guessed. He liked that about her and he'd find infinite ways to give her pleasure once he breached her maidenhead. After that, he would welcome the opportunity to explore all kinds of delights with her, and after this little display, he realized she'd be up for almost anything he could dream up.

Chapter Seven

Lana could hardly stop blushing long enough to dress in the gorgeous, green satin dress Candis had given her after that scandalous bath. The other knights left after Roland shot them a telling look, but Lana was still embarrassed by her total lack of inhibition. She couldn't believe she'd been so brazen, but Roland seemed to approve, so she tried to come to terms with the hussy she had surprisingly discovered within herself.

Smoothing the full skirt down her midriff and thighs, Lana looked up to find Roland watching her with hungry eyes. There was little doubt he liked what he saw. She was still apprehensive about what came next. She didn't quite know if she could handle what he would demand from her when Roland finally claimed her body with his. She was a virgin, after all, and she supposed almost all virgins had some fear of the unknown. But she trusted Roland. She trusted him with her life and would soon trust him fully with her pleasure. She was apprehensive, yes, but also eager for that final lesson, that initiation into the ways of love between a man and woman.

Would he want her now? Would he rush her to the nearest bedchamber and take his ease from her body? Or would he drag out her anticipation, tormenting her in this sharply exciting way, making her wonder when and where he would claim her body fully?

Roland kissed her lightly, and she knew it was the latter. Ushering her from the anteroom and into the hall, he touched her with polite hands that put her instantly more at ease. He was good that way, sensing when she was uncomfortable and doing what he could to make her feel more secure. He had a good heart, she realized, and didn't like to see her uncertain or embarrassed in front of others.

He was also the most handsome man she had ever seen. Tall, muscular and strong, his flashing green eyes heated her through and through. His dark hair had just a hint of wave to it, hanging long and healthy just above his shoulders. His face was angular and so masculinely beautiful, she had to stop herself from just staring at him and sighing. His wide shoulders and massive arms made her want to run her fingers all over him, learning his hard dips and valleys. The slight swirl of dark hair on his powerful chest made her want to explore his flat nipples and farther down his chiseled abdomen, down to the fascinating, mysterious hardness between his thighs.

She'd never seen a more magnificent male, not that she'd seen all that many cocks in her life, but she had glimpsed a few as the crude warriors of Salomar's house went about their business in public. None of those slovenly men had anywhere near the physique or massive man parts Roland boasted. His cock was thick and long, making her wonder just how he intended to fit it inside her untried body. The idea made her squirm in both fear and longing. She wanted to know, finally, what it felt like to be possessed by a man. By Roland. She knew she would never find any better man to take her virginity than Roland, and she looked forward to the event with both trepidation and a sort of hopeful anxiety.

Would it hurt? Would he be gentle and kind, or rough and impatient? She was betting he'd be as gentle as possible, judging by the way he'd already given her pleasure twice now, so unselfishly. She knew he had been left hard and wanting both times, but he'd made nothing of it, letting her know through his actions that all was well. He told her in no uncertain terms that he wanted her, but was showing her by his actions that he was a patient man who could wait for his pleasure until the time was right. He was like no man she'd ever known before and she counted herself lucky to know that sooner or later, this special man would be her first lover.

"I asked Hal, Jures and Candis to meet us in the great hall for an early supper." Roland spoke at her side as they walked down the wide hallway. "I want you to see the main hall and how we use it for meals and different events in the Lair, but I don't want to get bogged down in the ceremony of a formal state dinner—which we will if we don't sneak in before the crowd gathers. I hope you don't mind." He tucked her small hand into his arm, guiding her forward as he spoke.

"I prefer it, I think," she admitted. "Everyone's been staring at us and it's making me a little uncomfortable."

He shrugged. "You'll get used to it after a while, but I understand. You're new and puzzling to the knights, Lana. There are no female dragon riders here, and no Ice Dragons that I know of in the whole of the land. You'll have to get used to the attention. It should help to realize that they look on you and Tor with wonder, not enmity. You fascinate them, as you do me." He paused, running a light hand over her hair as he stared down into her eyes.

Moving closer, he made her feel like they were the only two beings in the entire world, so intimate did his caress feel on her hair. He bent to kiss her and the world narrowed even further to just the two of them, locked together in an embrace that felt so right, so pure, so loving, she couldn't question it. She could only revel in it as she returned his kiss wholeheartedly.

"Sire, don't you think you should do your courting in private?"

Hal's laughing voice came to her from out of the fog of sensual pleasure Roland had wrapped around her. She pulled back the little bit Roland would allow, her head clearing as she realized with shock they were in the middle of the crowded hall, people watching them from all sides. She found Hal, Jures and Candis smiling at them from just a few feet away and she just knew she was blushing furiously, but couldn't help it. Roland seemed not to mind at all. He just smiled and pulled her tight against his side.

"Mind your own business, Hal. Couldn't you see we were busy?" Roland's tone was stern, but his expression teased with good-natured humor.

"Any *busier* and we'd have found you pinning the poor girl to the wall." Hal's muttered observation made Roland's arm tighten around her waist, and she worried for a moment the knight had gone too far, but after just a few seconds, Roland relaxed and shook his head.

"Don't expect me to thank you for the interruption."

"You might not, but I bet your lady would." Hal winked at her and Lana couldn't help the little laugh that escaped her throat. The man was a true rogue. "Being older and wiser—and married—sire, I've learned a thing or two about the fairer sex. One being they don't always like being groped in a public hallway."

Sir Jures chimed in, tugging Lady Candis against his chest as he rested his head atop her soft curls. "And females have nasty ways of retaliating for any misstep on the part of their hapless mates, sire. Take it from one who knows."

Candis tried to reach around to pinch him, but Jures had her arms secured at her waist as she wriggled and giggled like a young girl. Lana was surprised by the change in the usually regal woman, being teased like a maid by her playful mates, and Lana knew there was deep and abiding love there, between all three partners to the odd union.

Roland laughed outright as Hal and Jures ducked in and kissed their woman, one on each cheek. Candis ceased to struggle and Jures let her go with another quick peck.

"I, for one, am rather hungry," Candis announced. "Shall we go in to dinner, Lana, and leave these men to loiter in the hall?" A conspiratorial wink accompanied her playful words and Roland let Lana slip from his grasp as she took Candis' hand. Daring greatly, Lana sent Roland a saucy wink over her shoulder as she and Lady Candis made their way, arm in arm, into the great hall.

The early dinner shared with the two knights and their mate was companionable and much less frightening than Lana had feared. Lady Candis made an effort to engage Lana in conversation and the knights seemed to truly respect her thoughts on the new weapons Salomar was using, once they put her at ease and broached the subject. Lana realized only after the meal was over that the knights were deeply worried about facing the weapons she and Tor had been learning to evade these past few seasons.

They agreed to meet in an hour, along with the weapons masters of the Lair to discuss the weapons in greater detail. Lana was glad for the chance to tell them what she knew. She feared Salomar would move before these knights and dragons were prepared. The sooner she told them everything she knew about the weapons, the more time they would have to train and equip themselves.

Roland put his arm around her as they walked together down the corridor after dinner. Most of the other knights in the Lair were just heading to the great hall, making little nodding bows to Roland as they passed. Farther away from the great hall, they encountered fewer and fewer people until finally they were alone in a suite of rooms she had never seen before.

"Aren't we staying with your friends tonight?"

"No, my dear. I asked Candis to arrange for us to have our own suite. Tilden and Rue will show Tor where we are when he's ready to come in. He should be here for the meeting as well. Some of the elder dragons will attend too, but I thought it might be easier for us, after our strategy session is out of the way, to be on our own."

So it would happen tonight. He would make love to her fully.

A thrill of anticipation laced with fear shot through her core, but she was ready. She wanted to know this man in every way, though fear of the unknown still plagued the recesses of her mind.

Lana shrugged, feeling just a bit shy, knowing what was to come later that night, though it remained unspoken. Better to concentrate on the more immediate future and the meeting that had been arranged. "I'm not used to being around so many people. Not to mention dragons."

"I know." He leaned down to place a kiss on the crown of her head. "You'll have to ease into it, and I know Tor will enjoy having the whole wallow to himself. He's such a big fellow, he needs the room."

She laughed lightly, feeling warm inside that he would take Tor's comfort into consideration. For that matter, she was warmed straight through to know he had given her feelings some thought as well. Roland showed her around the circular suite, explaining the uses of the various rooms, and before she knew it, the others were arriving for their little strategy session.

Roland stepped back to transform.

For Tor's benefit, he told her. *I'll stay near though, should you need me.*

Of the dragons, Tor bounded in first, plopping down in the center of the heated wallow and kicking up a little whirlwind of sand. Roland nodded toward a broom leaning against the curved wall and Lana took hold of it with a grin, sweeping the sand back into the pit indulgently as the baby dragon basked in its warmth. Rue and Tilden followed at a more sedate pace, taking the far end of the sand pit and sitting quietly while they welcomed two other adult dragons, one a deep, almost burgundy red, and the other with bright yellow gold scales.

Once Tor settled down and the sand was back where it belonged in the wallow, Roland, in dragon form, led Lana around to a grouping of chairs set by the widest part of the wallow. All the dragons craned their long necks to settle nearby, and it was quite obvious that was the place the meeting would be held so all present could participate—human and dragon alike.

Of the dragons, Roland was the most compact and well able to settle on the ledge with the human company, taking up a position just behind Lana's chair. It was clear both humans and dragons looked to him to lead this little get-together. He didn't disappoint.

Lana, may I present Ires and Kann, Roland indicated the dark red and golden yellow dragons in turn, *they are partners to Samnel and Josh, the weapons masters of this Lair.* As if on cue, two strange knights entered, making their way to the chairs and bowing respectfully to Roland. He extended the introductions to Tor and the newly arrived knights, and soon the group was assembled. Hal and Jures rounded out the group, and the meeting was underway.

Lana tried her best to answer all their questions about the various weapons she'd seen, evaded and fought against. The weapons masters asked astute questions, which Tor helped answer when she got stuck. She even found herself drawing pictures of some of the weapons, as best she could, on parchment the men had brought with them.

Tor took part too, explaining how each weapon performed and how he had managed to evade them. The dragons asked him detailed questions about his flight patterns and evasive maneuvers, and Lana was proud of the way he answered. She knew he was smart, but she was coming to realize just how intelligent he was for his age as she watched the older dragons and the way he so obviously impressed them. Roland rubbed up against her and she felt his warmth as they shared the special moment.

After more than an hour, the weapons masters seemed grimly content with the amount of information they'd been able to elicit. Lana was tired and thinking about the threat Salomar posed to these good knights and dragons worried her. Tor, she saw, was nearly asleep as the last of the dragons left, followed closely by the knights. As only the young can, he fell sound asleep between one breath and the next, and Lana was truly alone with Roland.

Her moment of truth had arrived at last. Lana knew what would probably come next and welcomed it. She felt like she'd waited forever for Roland and now he would be hers in every sense of the word—if only for that one moment in time when he joined his body to hers.

Roland transformed quickly and pulled her into his arms with a sharp, almost playful tug. She went without protest, surprised just a bit by his ardor as his mouth came down to claim hers. His tongue plunged deep as he moved with her toward the large bedchamber he'd shown her just briefly on their earlier tour. The doorway was open, an arch communicating directly to the wallow, like most of the rooms in the oval suite, but Tor was fast asleep, and their privacy was pretty much complete. When Roland had her backed up against the foot of the large bed, he lifted his mouth from hers, his eyes smoldering down at her.

"I can't wait any longer, sweetheart. I must have you now."

He punctuated his words with little biting kisses all over her face, chin and neck as his hands made short work of her pretty dress. Within moments, she was bare and lying across the bed.

"You are so beautiful, in every way. I want to savor you, my Lana, but I don't know if my will is strong enough. I want you too much."

"Roland, I—"

She didn't know what to say. Her head whirled but she knew and accepted that Roland would be her first lover, even though she still harbored some maidenly fears about what was to come. Lana had come to realize over the past days with Roland that no other man had ever—or would ever—mean as much to her as he did. He was special, a completely unique presence in her world.

She wanted to make love with him, even if it were just sex to him. She had no idea how he really felt about her, though she did think he had some special regard for both herself and Tor. Still, Roland was so handsome, so intelligent, and so highly ranked, and magical to boot, it would be foolish to think he might want something permanent with her, a mere runaway slave. She reconciled herself to taking what he offered without strings and without hope of a future together.

Though it broke her heart, she decided to live as much as she could in the moment with Roland. She would worry about tomorrow when it came. She might never have this chance again and she wanted to grab it with both hands. She wanted to grab *him* with both hands.

Reaching out, she ran her fingers over his strong muscles, emboldened when he growled low in his throat. The sound melted her bones and sent a shiver down her spine. While he kissed her, he did away with his clothing until she felt his hot skin, rough against hers. He felt so good as he broke the kiss and looked deep into her eyes, stroking her hair back from her face with a tender motion, so at odds with his obvious ardor.

"Tell me you want this, sweet Lana. Tell me you want me too."

"I do, Roland. I want you to be my first lover."

"Your only lover." He growled as she caught her breath but his fierce kiss cut off any question she might have put to him. She could barely think what he might mean by those fierce words. The look on his face was primitive as his lips slammed back down on hers with a force that could only be described as predatory.

His hands moved then, sweeping over her body with obvious, and delicious, expertise. For a moment she was jealous of his intimate knowledge of the female form but he made her feel too good to stay upset for long. He knew just how to play her, teasing her soft spots and lingering over the tight points that needed him so badly. He stroked her breasts and the delicate folds between her legs as if he owned her, and in that moment, she realized he probably did. He owned her passion, her unbridled response and—dare she admit—her heart.

"Spread your pretty legs for me, Lana. Spread them wide." His hot words whispered into her ear as he brought his heavy body over her. "Don't be afraid. I'll take good care of you."

"I'm not afraid of you, Roland, but I know it's got to hurt the first time."

He stilled, lifting away to look into her eyes. "I'll be as gentle as possible." His words were spoken in solemn tones and she was touched that this appeared to mean something to him besides a quick tumble. "It would kill me to hurt you, Lana. It would wound me deeper than a knife to cause you pain."

She sensed he was trying to say something, but the flames of her passion were stoked too high for anything to make much sense. Only him. That's all she needed. Roland, between her thighs, becoming one with her body, if only for a short span of time.

"Take me now, Roland. Please."

He cursed as he lowered his hips to rest between her legs. The struggle she read in the depths of his gaze let her know how hard he was trying to make this good for her. With renewed fervor he stroked her body, licking down her neck all the way to the points of her breasts, making her squeal as he bit down gently on her tight nipples.

"Are you hot for me, little Lana? Is the fire in your veins?" He whispered against her skin as his tongue licked into her belly button. She shivered, the muscles of her belly contracting sharply as a wave of pleasure rode through her.

"Roland, please!"

"In a moment, sweetling. First, I want to taste your fine nectar. You taste so good."

He swiped his tongue along the sensitive folds, lingering on her tight clit, catapulting her into orbit with one last push of his talented tongue. She spasmed in pleasure as he moved back up her body. Dimly she registered he was holding himself with one hand, guiding his long, hard cock to the place that was made for it in her body, but she was too far gone in pleasure to tense up as he probed gently at her entrance.

With steady pressure, he bore down on her, finding his way inside a little at a time. With rocking motions, he eased his passage into her heated channel until he came to the barrier that must be breached. When he would have backed off, she reached behind him with her feet, pulling herself up onto him, breaking the barrier with a little yelp of pain, her gaze locked firmly on his all the while.

Then he was through the barrier and there was nothing but pleasure on the other side. She held him deep and close, enjoying the odd sensation of fullness and rapture for the first time in her life. She thought she might finally understand why some of the women in Salomar's keep had done this with so many men. Still, she knew it was Roland who made this sharing of her body special and she couldn't imagine letting any other man within herself to this extent. Only Roland. For as long as he wanted her.

"Are you all right?" His voice was slightly harsh, his breathing accelerated.

She nodded, swallowing hard around her passion. "I'm fine. Oh, Roland, I never knew…"

He chuckled and she felt it within her core. "There's so much more I want to show you, my heart, so much more I want to give you." He began to move then, shuttling in and out slowly at first, driving the flames of her passion higher than she believed possible.

She'd thought the pleasure he'd shown her before was magnificent, but it was nothing when compared to what he did to her now. His hands stroked over her body as he moved within her, tugging at her nipples as his lips sought and found hers. He kissed her deep, his tongue stabbing into her mouth much like his cock sank into her pussy—over and over again. She moaned around his marauding tongue and was rewarded with a quick nip of her lower lip that made her squeak. He was a talented lover and he knew just how to stroke her to drive her higher and higher still.

When the pinnacle of pleasure was finally within sight she looked up at his handsome face, sensing him watching her. His gaze connected with hers, and she felt something shift and awaken deep inside her soul. Something breathed to life, some fire ignited, burning hot and low inside her that she'd never felt before. It was invigorating and it pushed her over the edge of sanity into the mindless oblivion of bliss.

She cried out as she came harder and longer than anything she'd known before. Within moments, she felt Roland stiffen within her and his hot seed shot into the deep recesses of her womb. She felt the fire of him and the answering fire rising within herself. She recognized him on some deep, unprecedented level. She'd been made for this, made for him.

His release went on and on, spurring her own. His seed sought purchase inside her and she prayed for a short moment it found a home within her womb and gave her a part of him to love and cherish forever as much as she loved him in this moment. If she could have nothing else of him, she wanted his child.

The thought was staggering.

As her eyes cleared, she found him watching her, the ragged breaths of his exertion bathing her face in warmth. His skin was hot to the touch, warming her deliciously wherever they touched while her insides were still blazing from his passion.

"Sweet Mother." The exclamation sighed out of her as she tumbled down from the greatest peak of pleasure she'd ever known.

Roland chuckled, leaning up on his elbows so as not to crush her.

"You are perfect for me in every way, my beautiful Lana. Tell me you'll be mine."

She nodded, tears gathering in her eyes. This was so much more than she'd dare hope for! He wanted to keep her for a while and she would take any amount of time he would spare.

"Yes, Roland. I'm yours for as long as you want me."

He smiled and hugged her close, rolling while still joined in the most intimate way. She rested on top of him, straddling his body while his fingers swept in long strokes over her back and down to her ass, squeezing her cheeks as she squirmed.

"You'd better get used to me, sweetheart, because I don't think there will ever come a time when I won't want you." Shock stopped her wiggling as she looked down into his brilliant green eyes. She held her breath at the serious gaze returned to her. "I love you, Lana. I want you with me always."

Tears fell then. Just a few, but she was helpless against them. He tenderly wiped her eyes with his broad fingers and she tried her best to smile for him. She was so happy, she thought she might burst.

"Oh, Roland! I love you too." Throwing caution to the wind, she kissed him, for the first time initiating intimacy between them. "I love you so much!"

He stiffened inside her again, and before she knew it, she was riding him to a quick, amazingly passionate climax. Her words of love poured out as she shattered in his arms. Rolling them so he could control her increasingly erratic movements, Roland rose over her. She gloried in his strength and the control he exerted over both of their bodies. He pumped into her hard and fast, bringing her to yet another climax, even higher than the last. She cried out as they reached the top together, spiraling downward, still together, holding each other tight.

"You are my heart, Lana." He breathed heavily into her hair as he held her closer than close. "Say you'll be my wife. Please, my love. Will you marry me?"

"Yes. Oh, yes, Roland."

She couldn't say anything more as the tears of joy overtook her once again, but he seemed to understand. He released her just enough so he could wipe her joyful tears with a corner of the bed sheet.

"You've made me the happiest of men." He kissed her tenderly and tucked her into his arms. "Rest now, my dearest love."

Chapter Eight

The next morning they got a bit of a late start. Lana and Roland breakfasted in the great hall while the older dragons watched over Tor's meal in preparation for the long flight ahead. Dragons didn't need, necessarily, to eat every day, but when they were young and still growing, like Tor, or expending a great deal of energy in a long flight, they needed more fuel for their fire. Tor would eat heartily of the herds reserved for dragonkind in this land under the guidance and tutelage of elders of his kind. That was a first and Lana could readily feel Tor's unabashed excitement, through their bond, to be flying with and learning from other dragons for the first time in his young life.

With Tor in the far pastures, happily chasing sheep, Roland lingered in his human form, teasing her senses and firing her newly awakened passions. Which was precisely why they were so late to breakfast and nearly everyone else had already departed the great hall to start their day.

When they entered the great hall hand in hand, amused looks followed Lana and Roland's progress to the tables that still held some remnants from the huge communal breakfast. Roland and she were able to collect at least enough of the savory dishes that were leftover for the two of them to enjoy an intimate meal.

Roland led her to a table in a far corner, where they were out of direct view of most of those who lingered in the hall. Despite his efforts, Hal and Jures found them not long after they'd sat down. The two knights seated themselves at the table with knowing looks and teasing smiles, but it was the irrepressible Hal, of course, who couldn't resist voicing the thoughts coursing through his mind.

"Late night, sire?" A raised eyebrow accompanied his question while Jures snorted and chuckled.

Roland didn't even dignify Hal's impertinence with a response, though Lana felt her cheeks heat with an uncontrollable blush. Hal only chuckled and shifted forward in his seat to try again.

"I know we often find it difficult to sleep the first night in a strange place. Perhaps next time you should try a sleeping drought. I'm sure Candis would be more than happy—"

"Leave off, Hal, you miscreant," Roland muttered with grumpy good grace as he tucked one strong arm around Lana's shoulders. "Can't you see you're embarrassing my lady?"

Hal was immediately contrite as he turned to her. "I'm just teasing our Roland, my lady. It's so good to see him whole and happy. All our people are indebted to you for that." The handsome knight's earnest words touched her.

"Pay us no mind, milady. It's Roland we make sport of. Not you," Jures assured her. "You are much too lovely to torment."

"Not to mention," Hal joked with a twinkle in his eye, "none of us want to get on the wrong side of your rather large-taloned protector."

She read genuine, affectionate respect in his words and couldn't help but like the mischievous, older knight. She sent him a smile as she finished the last of her morning tea.

"Tor and I look out for each other, but you're right—he's much better equipped for the role than I." She held up one dainty, albeit talonless, hand and chuckled. The knights followed suit as Roland captured her fingers, kissed the tips and tucked her little hand close against his heart.

"Ah, but your protection of our new young friend is even more precious, for you safeguard his heart." Jures' sensitive words brought an unexpected tear to her eye. "With your guidance, he's already grown to be one of the most beautiful souls I have ever encountered."

Hal broke the serious mood by slapping his friend on the back. "Ol' matchmaker here is hoping one day our little Rena will catch young Tor's eye as a potential mate."

Lana gasped. "But they're just babies!"

Jures shook his head with a smile. "Just a few more winters— quicker than a flash—and they'll be of age. No sense in not thinking ahead. It'd be a fine thing to have an Ice Dragon in the family, wouldn't it, Hal?" Jures sat back with a satisfied grin, apparently thinking far into the future, dreaming of his dragon daughter's triumphant match.

"It will all unfold as the Mother wills it, Jures. You know that." Roland chided the knight good naturedly.

"It never hurts to dream, sire." Jures winked at Lana, making her smile. The man had such an easy manner, it was hard not to like him.

"And if you're going to dream," Hal put in, "you might as well dream big, I always say. The bullies who tease Rena now will regret it one day when she's mated to the biggest, fiercest, shiniest, and kindest dragon in the land."

Lana loved the way Hal envisioned Tor when he was grown, and she leaned over the narrow table and placed a quick kiss on his cheek.

"Now why kiss him and not me?" Jures wanted to know. "I'm much handsomer than this ugly lug."

Lana was saved a reply by the arrival of Lady Candis.

"Have these two been misbehaving again?" Candis asked as she claimed a seat between her two knights, placing a basket before her on the table. "This is for you, Lana. For the journey." Candis pushed the straw basket toward her and Lana lifted the lid to find a wide selection of fruits, cheeses, breads, and sweets all packed neatly inside.

"Thank you." Lana felt tears gather behind her eyes again at the woman's kindness. It'd been so long since anyone had done anything for her out of the goodness of their heart. Only since Roland had entered her life like a whirlwind had such things been happening to her, and she was heartily unused to it. "You are too kind, truly, Lady Candis, to think of my comfort. I don't know what to say."

"You've already said it, my dear." Candis placed one hand briefly over Lana's and squeezed lightly. "And you're quite welcome. I hope we'll have a chance to visit again sometime. I've enjoyed meeting you and your lovely boy, Tor. He'll grow to be a fine dragon one day."

"And maybe you'll consider putting a good word in with him for our Rena, when the time comes." Jures sent her an exaggerated teasing wink and she couldn't help but laugh.

"Rena's beauty and charm speak for themselves, even now," she answered with what she thought was good diplomacy. "You can be very proud of her."

"Oh, we are." Hal stretched back in his seat.

Lana marveled at these humans who took such interest in the dragons who were part of their lives. "I can see that, and I'm glad to learn I'm not the only human who's as proud of her dragon baby as if he were my own child."

"Oh, that's natural among Lair families," Candis assured her, "since we all take a part in raising our young—whether human or dragon matters not. Tilden and Rue were just as proud of our sons, Jethry and Tod, when they were chosen as knights by Magus and Senti."

"I didn't know you had grown sons." Lana was surprised, indeed. Though Candis looked older, Lana didn't think the other woman was old enough to have two grown sons who were both knights with dragon partners of their own.

"And a daughter too," Hal winked. "She's the eldest and she just had her first child. A little girl."

"You're grandparents?" Lana was shocked.

The three chuckled good naturedly at her dismay and Roland squeezed her waist briefly as he laid his napkin aside and rose.

"Interesting as this is, we really need to get going, and I need to settle a few things before I take my other form."

The knights rose instantly when Roland stood and Lana read the respect in every line of their bodies toward her new lover. A warm ember blazed in her middle as she looked up at him, remembering the night of discovery they had shared. He was such a great man and it was obvious his friends loved and respected him in equal measure. That told her a lot about him, though her heart knew even without this proof that he was a wonderful man.

The three men moved off, talking among themselves, leaving Candis and Lana to follow at a slower pace. Candis fell into step next to Lana and she could feel the older woman's eyes on her.

"He is a very special man, Lana."

"I know."

"We've wondered for a long time how he would find a woman worthy of him. I'm glad to see that he finally has."

Lana was astounded by the woman's warm tone. They'd only just met, but already Candis seemed to really like her. Lana hadn't had any friends in her life—except for Tor, of course—but she liked Candis, and though she didn't quite know how to go about it, she wanted to be her friend if at all possible.

"You're very kind, Lady Candis," she said softly, unsure how to proceed. "I've enjoyed my time here among your family and making your acquaintance. If you meant what you said, I'd like…someday…to come back for a visit."

Candis stopped as they neared the landing area and shocked Lana by pulling her into a quick, almost motherly hug. "You're welcome here any time, Lana. Don't worry. I have a feeling this is only the start of a long and happy friendship. If I'm not much mistaken, Roland will make it so you visit often. He loves this Lair since he trained here as a young dragon. It's like his second home."

Lana dared to let herself dream that this wonderful fairytale she'd fallen into was real. Roland loved her. He'd told her so. But could such happiness really be hers? It didn't seem possible, but even Lady Candis—a woman she'd come to respect greatly—seemed to believe it.

Perhaps…just perhaps…it was.

Lana felt a kind of bubbly elation fill her soul at the idea. She hugged Lady Candis one last time as Roland beckoned to her. He was at the portal that opened onto the main landing platform of the Lair and she could see the early sun reflecting off Tor's shiny scales through the large opening. He was with the older dragons, twining necks with them in a dragonish farewell. Even he knew it would soon be time to go.

Roland pulled her in for a fierce hug and a devastatingly passionate kiss that drew a few low whistles from the knights who were still nearby. Lana was breathless when Roland finally released her.

"That'll have to hold us 'til we reach my home." He winked devilishly at her and she felt the impact of him in her womb and all the way down to her toes. The man was potent. That was a fact. He dragged her close to whisper in her ear. "When we reach the palace, I'm going to lock you in my chambers and ravish you for days. I'm going to show you ways of pleasure you've never imagined and I'm going to make you scream in delight. What do you think of that idea?" He pulled back enough to look down at her. His roguish smile was nearly her undoing as she felt her knees grow weak. "Well? What say you, my love?"

"I—" Her voice croaked and she had to clear her throat and try again. "I think that's a wonderful plan, Roland."

The smile he awarded her with promised of sensuous thrills ahead of which she could only dream. "Think of me while we navigate the sky today, lover. Think of me between your thighs, in your body, in your heart." His words were low and rugged, and for her ears only. "As I'll be thinking of your soft thighs and softer sighs. You hold my heart, Lana. Keep it safe."

"Roland," she reached up and placed her lips next to his ear, "I love you so much!"

He kissed her again until the "whoops" from the surrounding knights could no longer be ignored. Breaking apart at long last, he placed her a few feet from himself with deliberate, obviously difficult motions as the knights laughed at his predicament. Roland took their teasing with aplomb, laughing as much at himself as they did, and Lana found herself laughing with them, though her body was on fire with need. Only for Roland.

"Go to Tor now, love. I'll join you in a minute."

Lana squeezed his hand once more before turning and skipping off to where Tor waited, surrounded by other dragons. She was surprised and gratified to see little Rena closest to him. His sheltering wing protected the little one from the bigger dragons who crowded around him. He was such a thoughtful boy, always protecting those weaker or smaller than himself. The Mother knew he'd done as much for her time and time again.

Lana neared and saw Tor tentatively extending his long neck to twine with Rena's in the farewell he'd been taught, while Rue and Tilden looked on with what could only be described as indulgent expressions. Perhaps all that chatter at breakfast wasn't just idle speculation. Perhaps there was an attraction there, though the dragonets were much too young to even understand what might prove to ultimately be a lifelong partnership.

Lana didn't like thinking about what would happen when Tor was old enough to mate and form a family of his own. She didn't want to think about what that would mean to her. She was happy as it was now, and content to let each day pass as it would without borrowing troubles from tomorrow. Still, seeing the two youngsters twining necks so prettily, she wondered if maybe she wasn't seeing a foreshadow of the future.

Roland met them on the ledge in dragon form so as to preserve the secret from young Tor and the other dragonets present, but Lana knew sooner or later, Tor would be let in on the secret of Roland's amazing dual nature. It was Roland's secret to tell though, and Lana respected his right to pick the time and place.

Tor moved away from the other dragons and bent one foreleg so she could climb aboard his back as they had done many times over the years they'd been together. Lana adjusted her furs, though she needed less and less covering to keep her warm the farther south they flew. She felt the curious eyes of the knights and their families—many of whom had gathered on the landing ledge, apparently to see them off—on her as she climbed easily aboard Tor's broad back.

Ready, friends? Roland's distinctive voice sounded through her mind and she knew he addressed Tor as well.

Ready, Roland! Tor, eager and happy, answered back.

And what about you, my love? Roland sent the words to her alone on their private pathway. *Are you ready?* The purr in his deep voice implied he was talking about more than flying.

Lana decided to be daring. *I think I'm always ready for you, Roland.*

Now that's *what I like to hear!* Roland leapt into the air with renewed vigor after blinking one big emerald eye in Lana's direction. She giggled and held on tight as Tor launched into the air with joyful abandon. The dragons behind them roared and trumpeted in farewell, a few flying out as honor guard with them for the first leg of the journey.

It was a beautiful day for flying.

By sunset they had stopped a few times to allow Tor to rest, and Lana had eaten a bit of the food Candis had thoughtfully packed for her. Roland took Tor to hunt sheep in the pastures set aside especially for dragons, watching over the dragonet as he learned. Roland instructed him on which sheep were eligible for eating and the various marking systems the shepherds and farmers used in order to keep their flocks and herds organized. The markings allowed the farmers to not only select which animals were set aside for the dragons, but also to receive payment for each animal from the king's treasury.

The system allowed both dragons and farmers to flourish, and Lana was impressed by it all. Tor had learned the rudiments rather quickly from the older dragons at the Lair that morning, but he also seemed to enjoy Roland's patient tutelage about the different markings on the flocks as they traveled southward. Lana realized by watching them that Roland was a kind and generous teacher. He would probably be a wonderful father, she found herself thinking, realizing she could very well already be carrying his child.

She pondered the amazing idea as they retook to the sky on what Roland promised would be the last leg of their journey.

Would their child be human or dragon? Or both? Her eyes went wide at the possibilities. She had not fully considered the possible consequences when she'd welcomed him into her arms and body last night, but the idea was heating her insides as she thought about it now. When they were married, they would have babies, she hoped. She wondered how many he would want, and most importantly, would they be part dragon, able to change like him? The very idea of it boggled her mind.

The faraway trumpeting of dragons drew her attention and she looked up in time to see two black specks in the distance growing steadily larger as they neared. They resolved into two black dragons, only slightly different in appearance from Roland. Their welcome was unmistakable as they circled around to flank Roland, grazing wings in welcome. The pair of them took up escort positions, one on either side of Roland and Tor, though both sets of peridot eyes were looking at Tor…and Lana.

The two new black dragons were like mirror images of each other and they shared traits with Roland as well. The only real difference was their lighter green eyes. They watched her and Tor carefully but made no move to communicate that she could discern, except perhaps with Roland. She would bet the three black dragons were talking at great length back and forth among themselves.

In a way, it was a repeat of what had happened when the Northern Lair's sentries spotted them coming over the border. Except of course this time, their dragon escorts were riderless and the dragons were pure black. Knowing what she knew about Roland, she surmised these dragons might also be the kind that could shapeshift into men. Keeping that in mind, she watched them speculatively.

She was so busy looking at the two new black dragons, she almost missed her first glimpse of the royal palace as they came over the last of the mountains standing in their path. The castle was enormous, seemingly carved into the living rock of yet another mountain. Spires rose into the sky on all sides and little corkscrew roads were carved into the lower levels of the mountain, meandering down to grassy hillsides teeming with sheep, cattle, horses and crops, and a city spread out below.

It was absolutely breathtaking.

Do you think that's where Roland lives? Tor asked in an awed tone, his words for her alone. *It's even bigger than the Lair and I never thought I'd see anything better than that!*

This is where the king lives, Tor. It's the royal palace, a castle built into the mountain so that dragons and people can live together there in comfort. She repeated a bit of what Roland had told her the day before. *I think this is probably the grandest Lair in all of Draconia.*

I guess it would have to be if the king lives here, huh?

Yes, I guess so. She stroked his neck fondly as his massive wings beat around her. How she loved flying with Tor. She would never grow tired of the magic of being higher than most birds, nearly touching the clouds. She only hoped the king would let her continue to be with Tor as he grew and learned from the dragons of this new land.

As they drew nearer to the amazing castle she saw the tall spires were actually quite a bit larger than she'd expected. Each was big enough to accommodate the take-off and landing of a dozen dragons at any one time. In fact, there were many dragons in the air around the castle and she noted a few awaiting them on the wide ledge of the nearest spire as they moved in for a landing.

As the other dragons saw them, they began to trumpet greetings all around. Soon a large bell began to toll somewhere below and she was amazed by the extent of the welcome. Intellectually, she knew Roland was an important person to the people and dragons of this land, but the warm, joyous welcome still surprised her.

The two new black dragons held back to let Roland land first, then Tor. They set down behind Tor, almost as if they were the rear guard. Lana couldn't help but shoot looks behind her as she dismounted from Tor's back, watching the twin blacks watch her. If they were trying to intimidate her, they were doing a good job.

Feeling scared for no reason soon annoyed her. Lana squared her shoulders as she removed her travel pack from Tor's back and dropped it to the ground. Rubbing his shoulders almost absently, she turned to face the two new blacks. They were still watching her and she'd had enough of it. Facing them, Lana put her hands on her hips as Tor stood behind her.

Thank you for the escort, she said belligerently into their minds, easily including Tor and Roland in her silent speech, *but you can stop eyeing us as if we're the enemy. Roland wouldn't have brought us here if we weren't to be trusted.*

In fact, Roland stepped forward, moving his massive body between her and the other dragons, *I wouldn't even be alive if it weren't for them.*

Then we owe you a debt we can never repay, the one on the right said with a wicked, dragonish grin. The one on the left seemed amazed she would bespeak them directly.

You're a girl! That came a moment later from the one on the left as she took off her head covering. All of them laughed at his surprise, and if dragons could blush, she knew he was doing so.

The genius on the left, Roland said wryly, *is my brother Darius. His evil twin, on the right, is Connor. Please excuse their rude behavior. They were just leaving.*

But, Rol! We've never met an Ice Dragon before. Don't chase us off just yet. Darius seemed to recover his equilibrium.

Roland limited his words to Lana and the twins. *He may be an Ice Dragon, but he's just a baby, only five winters old, and he'd never seen another dragon before he met me a few days ago. Go easy on him, boys. He has a gentle, trusting heart.*

Lana was touched to hear him describe Tor with such feeling. The other two dragons seemed to realize his seriousness and looked at Tor with new, kinder eyes.

So he doesn't know about us. Connor watched the tired dragonet stretch, his icy scales glistening brilliantly in the final rays of the setting sun.

No. Not yet. Roland confirmed. *But Lana knows.* His long neck swiveled to her, his eyes looking down on her with emerald glints.

Lana? Connor prompted, his voice tinged with interest.

Princess Alania of Kent, if I'm not mistaken, Roland confirmed, shocking her with the strange title, *my fiancée.*

Stunned silence met his announcement and Lana began to feel awkward, but she kept her spine straight and tried not to let her discomfort show.

Roland— Connor began, only to be cut off by Darius.

That's great! His joy was so real, Lana felt herself begin to relax.

Congratulations, Roland and to you, milady. Connor's tone was more serious.

Tor doesn't know about that yet, either, Lana said quickly as her baby's great silver head loomed over her shoulder. She patted and stroked his cheeks, smiling as he butted into her affectionately.

I'm Tor. He was clearly tired from their long flight that day, but wanting to meet the new dragons. Introductions were made quickly and then Roland led the party down a wide, sloping hall leading to an inner ledge. Lana remounted for a quick flight downward within the magnificent inside walls of the remarkable castle.

Roland had picked up Lana's pack in one front paw and held it now as he led the group off the ledge, spiraling down in wide circles to a well-protected inner courtyard. Lana dismounted again and was immediately enchanted by the trickling waterfall on one side of the secluded court.

Roland strolled through a wide set of double doors opened by two attentive servants as he approached. Tor had to duck his head a little, but once inside the massive corridor, he walked comfortably among the smaller dragons. Decorative tapestries of every color hung here and there on the walls, and the floors were polished smooth and made of the native stone. Lana was impressed by the understated opulence of the huge corridor but the suite they entered a moment later truly took her breath away.

Like the Lair she had visited in the north, it boasted a large, oval sand pit that radiated warmth. Tor jumped in with gleeful delight as Roland told him this was his room for as long as he stayed in the castle.

He commenced to rolling around, polishing his scales the way the dragons at the Lair had taught him, to a blinding brilliance.

And I thought he was sparkly before! Darius commented as they watched him indulgently. Within moments, he was as clean and brilliant as polished crystal.

Lana approached the edge of the sand pit, sitting down on the ledge near Tor's large head. He was so tired, he was nearly asleep as he let her caress him behind the eye ridges, growling a little in pleasure.

"Go to sleep, baby. You're safe here and we'll be nearby." She looked to Roland for confirmation.

Lana must bathe and eat, but my brothers will stay near if you need anything, Tor. If you want Lana, just tell one of them and I'll bring her right back, all right?

All right, Roland. Tor said sleepily around a smoky yawn. *Goodnight.*

"Goodnight sweetheart. Happy dreams." Lana left off stroking as Tor fell fast asleep.

I expect one of you to be with him at all times. He's very special to Lana and to me, and he's never lived anywhere but in captivity or a cold, snowy cave before a few days ago.

Poor little one, Connor said softly as he looked at the sleeping dragonet. *We'll watch over him, Rol. Go take care of your lady.*

Our soon-to-be sister, Darius added with a grin. *Hot damn, Rol! You do move quickly.*

Roland swooped his dragon head down to lick her neck with his slender tongue and she squeaked, swatting at him playfully. *When you see what you want, there's little reason to dither.*

Spoken like the tyrant you are. Connor grunted smokily as they laughed at their brother.

Watch your tongue or I'll have you thrown in the dungeon.

Wouldn't you rather take her there? It would be much more fun, I'm sure. Darius winked one sparkling, peridot eye at her outrageously and she had to chuckle even though she didn't quite understand the joke. She made a mental note to ask Roland later what was so funny about dungeons. From what she knew of Salomar's icy dungeon, it was no laughing matter at all, but perhaps customs were different here in this land.

They left Tor to the guardianship of his brothers, but when she expected Roland to lead her out of the large suite, he instead took her to one of the smaller rooms adjoining the dragon's wallow. The only real design difference in this suite from those of the Northern Lair that Lana could see was that the rooms leading off the wallow here had ornately carved doors that could easily be closed to ensure privacy.

Roland closed the door with a decisive swish of his tail, taking only a moment before changing to human form, wearing nothing at all. Lana caught her breath at his magnificence. She didn't think she would ever get used to his beautiful warrior's body.

He swept her into his arms and hugged her close. His lips found hers in a hungry kiss that lasted long, long moments while he began tugging at her clothing. When he let her up for air, she was gasping at the intense fire that ignited so quickly between them.

"I've been wanting to do that all day."

She giggled as his big hands fumbled with the little closures on her tunic and pants. Batting his hands away playfully, she did the job herself, but he wouldn't let her alone, tugging the tunic over her head even before the last tie was undone.

He placed nibbling kisses on the skin he exposed, starting with her tummy and working his way up to her breasts, pausing there to soothe the reddened tips with long strokes of his wet tongue. Lana shivered and gasped as he pleasured her, wanting him even more now she knew the bliss he could bring her.

He pushed the pants down her legs and lifted his head, bracing her with his arms as she stepped out of the tangled puddle of clothing. He scooped her up and placed her in the ornately carved stone pool. It was filled and waiting for them. The water was lukewarm, but as he placed his hand in and winked at her, it heated rapidly.

"Sometimes it's good to be a dragon." His devilish smile teased her as he picked up a tray from a side table and placed it on the wide rim of the stone pool.

"That's a nice trick, Roland. Why don't you come into the water and warm me some more?" She could hardly believe she spoke the daring words, but the leaping flames in his eyes were reward enough for her boldness. She knew he was eager, but was moving slowly for some reason. He sat on the stone ledge and lifted a pot of sweet smelling herbal salts, dumping them into the water with a small flourish, a soft expression on his hard features.

"I know after last night, and the long ride this morning, you've got to be a little sore." He added a soothing oil blend to the heated water that instantly calmed her slightly abraded skin. He'd been just a little rough with her the night before, but she'd loved every moment of it. Still, her sore nipples and the lingering ache between her thighs were nothing compared to the fire of her desire. She wanted him. No, she needed him. It was an emotional requirement, a physical ache, that she take him into her body and express the love in her heart in the way he had taught her.

"I'm not too bad," she insisted, moving her hand out of the water to rest daringly high up on his thigh. "Come into the water, Roland. I'm well enough for what we both want."

"No, my love." He bent to kiss her sweetly before reaching for another colorful vial on the tray. "This is my time to take care of you." He poured a small portion of sweet-smelling soap onto the crown of her head and created lather with soothing, circular strokes of his big fingers in her mass of auburn hair.

"Nobody's ever washed my hair before. Well, not since my mother, when I was a little girl. That feels so good."

Her eyes closed as he chuckled, urging her to lean back against his hard thigh. She drifted while he stroked through her hair and down farther over her neck and shoulders, relaxing her so thoroughly she started a little when he stopped to rinse out the fragrant herbal soap.

When her hair was clean and free of suds, he urged her to move forward a bit on the stone ledge carved into the side of the bathing pool. With a small splash, he entered the water behind her, pulling her hips back to settle in the cradle of his. She felt his hardness against her ass, settling into the seam as if he belonged there. The thought warmed her. She was new to love, but she knew without a doubt she wanted Roland beside her, inside her, as often as possible, for the rest of her days. He was part of her now even after so short a time together. It just was. There was no shadow of question in her mind.

He began to rub her shoulders and down lower with slippery herbal soap, digging into the muscles that needed it as if he knew her body better than she did herself. She chuckled as she realized he probably did. He had mastered her body so easily and so well, it would respond to his lightest whisper of touch.

"What are you thinking that puts such a dreamy expression on your lovely face?" His words breathed into her ear as she settled back against his muscled chest with a sigh.

"I was just thinking how good you are at this."

"I won't claim lots of practice. I've never wanted to pamper a woman the way I do you."

"Why not?" She stretched sinuously against him as he stroked her body.

He shrugged slightly. "No other woman has ever mattered this much to me before."

She snuggled in deeper to him, smiling. "While I don't enjoy hearing about all the other women you've had, I do sense a compliment in there somewhere, so you're forgiven."

He chuckled as he cupped her breasts, going easy on the slightly reddened nipples, rubbing in the soothing herbal compound, making them feel better. In fact, her whole body felt better under his touch. She thought she felt a slight tingle of healing energy as well, but dismissed the thought from her mind as he delved lower, distracting her.

"I'm of royal blood, sweetheart. Women have been throwing themselves in my path for a long time, and I'll admit I took them up on their offers more often than I probably should have. But never have I felt about any woman the way I feel about you, and I can promise you this—I'll never touch another woman as long as we live. Only you, Alania, my love, for the rest of our days."

He kissed her shoulder then, slipping his hands down in the warm water, stroking lightly over her tender skin. She wiggled closer to him as he sought her most tender spots.

"Roland." His name left her lips on a breathy moan as his fingers slid into the folds at the apex of her thighs. "Roland, please."

"Do you want me, my love? Can you take me? I don't want to hurt you."

She turned in the water to face him, allowing her legs to float up around his waist as she straddled his hard body.

"I want you, Roland." She held his gaze with her own. "I love you."

Groaning, he clasped her tightly, bringing his mouth to hers in a passionate, fiery kiss. The water around them steamed as their temperatures rose, the dragon in his soul waking to join once more with its mate.

"You're so perfect for me in every way." He laid her back over one strong arm as his hand delved down into the water, teasing her excitement higher and higher.

"Please, Roland, don't make me wait any longer. I need you now."

"As my lady wishes."

Roland turned her in the water, positioning her against one of the smoothly carved ledges, her bottom facing him. She looked over her shoulder with a questioning glance, but he stroked her shoulders and moved her body just the way he wanted it. He surged forward in the water, splashing it up over her back, the surface teasing her hanging nipples, and she wiggled to dip them in and out of the warmth of the water.

After a few moments more of his playful torture, driving her passion higher, he positioned himself at her entrance and pushed slowly but firmly within. She moaned as he slid in halfway, the tenderness of her newly awakened body forgotten in the ecstasy of his possession. He pulled slightly out and then pushed back in again. The slipperiness of the water and her own wetness helped him glide within, taking her fully.

"How does that feel?" He paused to ask, his hands stroking her back lovingly.

"Don't stop."

Her breathless cry seemed to spark his passion. He began to move with increasing speed and depth, rocking into her from behind and hitting a spot within her that sent her senses reeling. He possessed her utterly, demanding a response from her writhing body she hadn't known she could give. She began to stroke back against him, enjoying the coolness of the air on her torso, the warm lap of the water on her breasts and lower, and the incredible fullness of his possession within her core.

"Come with me, my love, come with me now."

His words spurred her on, breaking the wave that had been building until she cried out, keening. Her release went on and on. She felt him burst inside her, his hot essence shooting up into her womb, warming her to the core. When her knees threatened to buckle, his strong arms came around her waist to hold her bottom tight against him while he jerked once more within.

"Roland!" she gasped as a massive orgasm enveloped her.

"Lana, my love." He kissed her ear, biting down gently on the lobe, and sent another wave of pleasure through her as he continued to pump, softer now, inside her.

He held her for long moments as the pleasure crested, then gradually dissipated. Lana was like no woman he had ever known before. She pulled a response from within his soul, his heart, his very being, and the satisfaction he found with her was greater than anything he had ever dreamed could exist. She was his perfect match, his mate, his queen.

He drew out of her body slowly, oddly pleased when she protested the loss of his cock with a little whimper. Sitting on the ledge of the stone pool, he tugged her into his arms, locking tight around her. He would never let her go, never give her up. She was his.

Damn, Rol. She's beautiful.

Roland looked up to find his brother, Nico, standing in the shadows across the room. This bath chamber was designed with two entrances—one from the wallow and one from the servant's hall. He knew instinctively which entrance his brother, aptly called the Prince of Spies, had used.

She's mine.

Roland knew that simple warning was enough. Nico and he were only a year apart in age and very close friends. They had been partners in mischief as boys and shared many questionable exploits as teens and young warriors. They'd even shared women a time or two more than they probably should have, but then, neither had met a woman who mattered to them more than as just a night of sexual relief.

Until now.

She's the one, then? Nico asked, cocking his head at the woman who was still unaware of his presence.

Roland stroked her hair, settling her back against his shoulder, noting her closed, sleepy eyes and dreamy expression. She was so beautiful.

I love her, Nic. Roland knew Nico understood the importance of that statement. *She'll be my queen.*

So I'd heard. Nico nodded, a smile in his sparkling eyes, *I just wanted to see for myself.*

Did you get a good look? The teasing in his tone assured Nico knew he wasn't angry about his spying.

More than adequate, my liege, Nico teased back, and Roland knew there were no hard feelings on either side. *I'll leave you to it then.*

Stay. I'll introduce you.

Nico seemed surprised. *You think she'll be all right with that? She* is *naked after all. Most women wouldn't take kindly to meeting their new brother-in-law for the first time while in the bath after a hard fuck.*

I think you'll be surprised. She's still new to this, but after a while, I think she'll be up for anything I might ask of her. I already know for a fact she likes to be watched. Roland stroked her shoulders, shifting her in his lap. Her eyes opened and he kissed her long and deep.

Damn, Rol, she's a hot one, isn't she? Nico whistled through his teeth, deliberately alerting her to his presence.

Roland pulled back, gauging her reaction. She seemed surprised and a little nervous, but not frightened. He liked that.

"Sweetheart, this is my brother, Nico." He watched her closely as he made the introductions. The flaring of her eyes as Nico moved forward to stand near the wide rim of the pool indicated excitement and maybe just a hint of fear. "Nic, this is Lana."

Nico took Lana's hand from the rim of the pool and raised it to his lips, kissing her knuckles with a wicked grin. She shivered as Nico winked. The man was devastatingly handsome in a rakish sort of way, and his eyes, while green, were the deep hazel green of tourmaline rather than Roland's emerald. Still, the resemblance between the two brothers was easy to see. Both were tall, muscular and had firm features that spoke of strength both of body and of character.

"The pleasure is all mine. Congratulations, brother." Nico's knowing gaze raked over her body, or at least what he could see of it in the sudsy water. "Your mate is lovely and, from all reports, a remarkable woman."

"What are they saying about her, Nic?"

Roland's lazy question invited his brother to stay and chat. Lana was surprised, but as Roland stroked her under the water, she felt her body heat at the idea of two men watching her reactions. She shocked herself with the realization, much as she had in the Northern Lair when all those knights had been watching them.

Nico sat negligently on the wide rim of the stone pool, trailing the fingers of one hand lazily through the water. His hand came near, but never quite touched her skin. Still, the idea of it made her nipples stand up at attention.

"They say she's a dragon tamer and some claim she's a wild woman, but others talk of how she stole your heart with her Northland magic. The general consensus is that she'll keep you on your toes and make you the happiest of men—in the bedchamber and out. Rumors from the north say she's adventurous sexually," Lana gasped and Nico winked audaciously at her, "and very responsive to you. I see that part, at least, is truth."

Roland stroked his hands possessively over her breasts, cupping them and squeezing, showcasing her excited nipples. The fire within her was rising higher, burning hotter as Prince Nico's eyes followed every movement.

"You have no idea, Nic."

Roland's teasing laughter brought her wide eyes up to his. He took a moment to kiss her deeply, turning her in his arms to hug her tight. She rested her head on his shoulder while the men talked. Roland stroked her skin, his hands teasing everywhere as he and his brother discussed travel plans. She dimly heard Nico say he was leaving immediately for the new Border Lair and lands beyond, but Roland's daring fingers distracted her, plunging deep in her channel as she tried desperately to hold in her gasp.

She heard Nico chuckle and her eyes opened, her head turning to see fire in the dragon prince's eyes. The same fire burned in Roland's eyes and in her own soul.

"Roland."

Her whispered plea was torn from within as Roland stroked her higher. Nico stood just as Roland shifted her on his lap, bringing his cock right up inside her while his brother watched. The shock of it made her groan as she buried her face in her lover's corded neck.

"Fuck her good, Rol," she heard Nico say in a low voice. "I'll leave you to it."

"Good hunting, Nic." Roland grunted as he began pistoning in and out of her tight channel. She felt Nico's gaze linger on them for quite some time before he finally left, but by that time, she was too far gone in her pleasure to really notice.

Chapter Nine

"Do I look all right?" Lana smoothed the fine fabric of her dress over her curves, communicating distress in her every nervous twitch.

"You're beautiful." Roland squeezed her close and kissed her forehead gently. "They will love you as much as I do." He felt her nervousness as she trembled in his embrace. "Are you ready, or do you need a moment?"

Lana took a deep breath as he stepped back. She squared her shoulders and stared straight ahead at their objective—the ornate archway that led to the throne room. "I'm ready."

Roland nodded decisively and ushered her through the large portal. It was large enough for at least two dragons to walk abreast. He was so proud of her as she walked, straight and fearless at his side. She would be a great asset to his country and his people. Her heart, her courage and her sense of honor were deeply ingrained in the lovely, caring woman she was. All of those qualities, and her quick humor and even quicker wit, made him love her. She would be just the kind of wife he needed and the right woman to mother their children. Not to mention the fact he desired her above every other female he had ever known. Making those children would be no hardship. No hardship at all.

A loud gasp sounded from off to their right and he turned to find a lovely, older woman and a younger female, made in her image. Both were in tears as they looked at Lana. He followed their gazes to the beauty at his side and saw she was white as a sheet, her gorgeous eyes wide, gasping in shock.

He rubbed her back. "It's all right, sweetheart. Breathe, Lana."

She hiccupped a bit, smiling up at him for a split second before her gaze went again to the two women who waited just a few yards away. Lana's spine firmed under his stroking hand and she stepped forward.

"Are you...?" She faltered, moving slowly toward the younger woman who was moving to meet her. "Are you called Lora?"

The girl smiled widely. "Not since I was little. My name is Belora but my older sisters used to call me Lora. Which one are you?"

"I'm Lana."

"Alania!" The older woman gasped loudly as her tears flowed. "My baby."

The younger girl held out her hand and Lana took it. She was drawn forward to the older woman. Both were trembling with emotion.

"Mama?"

"Yes, my darling child!" The older woman flung her arms around Lana, hugging her close for a long, long, joyous moment. Belora hugged them both, piling on for a weepy group hug.

Roland joined the four knights standing off to the side, watching. He knew most of them quite well and shook hands with Gareth and Lars, pausing a moment by the older men to renew his acquaintance with Lord Darian—formerly of Skithdron—and his new fighting partner, General Jared Armand.

"Lord Jared, I've missed you," Roland said with a genuine smile. "Congratulations on your wedding, and you, Lord Darian." He turned to face the foreign man. "I want you to know Draconia thanks you for your actions in coming over to our side. My brother, Nico, gave me detailed reports of your actions and all that you risked to keep our people and our dragons from slaughter. You have my personal thanks, sir, and a boon should you ever need it. Just ask."

"Thank you, sire."

Darian had a warm, generous smile and Roland remembered the former ambassador. Roland had known him when he was just a lad, watching the court from the sidelines. He'd always liked the rakish foreigner and had missed him when he left for home after several years at his father's court.

"So I guess the four of you are prince-consorts now," Roland said with a teasing smile. "Welcome to the royal family."

Gareth gave him a sheepish grin. "I had no idea our Belora was a princess when Kelvan and I found her in the forest. This prince-consort thing is going to be hard to get used to, sire."

All the men chuckled at that, and a moment later, the women rejoined them, still a little moist-eyed, but their faces lit with wide, happy grins. Belora moved to stand between her two knights, drawing them forward to meet her newfound sister.

"This is Gareth," she motioned to the darker-haired knight on her right, "and this is Lars." He was more somber and blond-headed. "They're my mates."

Lana's eyes sparkled as her lips curved with a grin. "Married already? Way to go, little sis."

The men chuckled and Gareth winked over at Lars, both of them moving in concert to plant smacking kisses on both of Lana's cheeks at once. Their coordinated moves made all of them laugh.

"Welcome home, Princess Alania," Gareth said as he drew back, putting one strong arm around his wife, while Lars settled one hand around her hip on the other side.

"Princess?" Lana looked over at Roland. "I'm really not a princess."

Roland stepped up to her, putting one strong arm around her waist and pulling her close.

"Actually, you *are* a princess, by right of blood. The House of Kent—your House, my love—is of royal blood and breeds true, which means all the members of the Kent line are considered princes or princesses of the realm. You, your mother and your sisters all gained the title princess at birth." He squeezed her tight, knowing what he would say next would come as a shock. "But when you marry me, you will be queen."

"What?" She was breathless in his arms and he tightened the embrace just a bit, to comfort and support her.

"I'm the king, sweetheart, and you will be my queen."

"Sweet Mother of All!"

Before she could faint, Lana felt a soft touch on the back of her head and a small rush of healing energy flowed into her, settling her feet back firmly on the ground. She looked around and realized her mother had reached out to prevent her from swooning with a quick, healing touch. She remembered that warm, tingly feeling from her youth.

"Thanks." Her eyes swiveled back to Roland—make that *King* Roland—she felt faint again, but swallowed hard to keep from giving in to the feeling. "Why didn't you tell me?"

"I'm telling you now." He grinned in a totally satisfied male way that made her insides itch.

"I mean before now." She pulled back from him a bit. "Don't you think I'd be interested to know that Tor and I were consorting with a *king?*" Her voice rose with each word, as did her panic. "Stars! Roland, how could you even consider asking me to marry you? I'm a runaway slave. I know nothing about being a queen or even a princess for that matter."

He tried to soothe her, running one large hand gently over her hair. His eyes were so loving, so caring, and she felt so safe in his arms, but still her panic rose.

"Nevertheless, you are a princess, and you'll be my queen." His voice was pitched low, for her ears alone, it seemed. "I love you, Lana. There is no other woman in this world for me. If you don't marry me, I'll live out my days alone. You wouldn't sentence me to that misery when we can be so happy together, would you?" He hugged her close, whispering in her ear. "I need you, Lana. Only you. Please don't be afraid."

All her arguments crumpled in the face of his need. She felt his big body trembling just slightly against her. She loved him so much!

Softly, she reached up and kissed his jaw, then his cheek. "I don't think I can handle being queen," she said softly, "but I do want to be with you, Roland. I don't think I could live without you now."

He hugged her and she became aware of the people watching them. Backing up, a slight flush pinkened her cheeks.

"Um…" She looked around, her expression sheepish, and Roland chuckled at her hesitancy.

He turned, keeping one arm around her shoulders as he faced the group once more.

"Don't be embarrassed, child, we're your family." Her mother's voice was so warm, so welcome, Lana felt the tears start behind her eyes again, but she wouldn't let them fall.

"I just never thought I would ever have a family again." Without her volition, her voice trembled and Roland squeezed her shoulders.

"Well, now you'll have more family than you ever bargained for, my love." Roland's eyes sparkled as he looked at her. "Just here, we have two sets of knights and their dragon partners are outside even now, becoming acquainted with our boy, Tor."

"Tor?" one of the older knights, flanking her mother, asked. He had kind eyes and she liked the love and respect in his gaze and his manner as he stood so close at her mother's side.

She would have explained who Tor was, but Roland stopped her with one finger over her lips and a teasing smile. "No, I think they need to see this for themselves." He cocked his head as if listening to something only he could hear and she realized he was probably in communication with his brothers. "They'll be here shortly. In the meantime," he turned to the older set of knights, "you haven't been introduced to your new stepfathers yet."

She gasped as she realized the implications of his words. She remembered her own father only dimly. He'd died when she and her twin were still little, but these two men, one on either side of her mother, were smiling and kind. They were also fierce warriors, not old, but their eyes held a calm wisdom she could respect.

The one with the scar running down his face stepped forward. "I'm Jared." He took her hand in his, giving it a warm, welcoming squeeze. A smile turned his face from fierce to friendly in the blink of an eye. "And this is Darian." He relinquished her hand to the other man, who was spectacularly handsome in a rakish sort of way.

"You are as lovely as your mother, and your pretty sister." Darian winked as he kissed her hand gallantly. She liked both men and liked even more the way they treated her mother.

"I married these two," Adora said with a hint of a blush in her pretty face, "just a short while ago." She moved between the two men and both put an arm around her lovingly. "Do you remember a dragon I used to tell you stories about when you were little? Her name was—"

"Kelzy!" Lana piped in with a smile. "I remember the stories you used to tell us. The adventure tales about Lady Kelzy and how you would ride on her foot when you were just a toddler. I think that's why I was never truly afraid of Tor." She turned to Roland with a joyous light in her eyes, but her attention was captured by the entrance of what seemed like a long line of dragons.

She was entranced by their colors and shine, as well as their size. They were larger than Tor, but not by much. These were adult dragons, she knew, and each one of them stopped before her, forming a semi-circle around her and Roland. Their heads bowed low in respect as Roland nodded to each in turn and their jeweled eyes fixed on her.

"My love, this is the rest of your family. Rohtina, partner to Lars." He indicated a lovely golden female dragon with reddish highlights, then moved to a sparkly blue-green dragon at her side. "And her mate, Kelvan, partner to Gareth." She acknowledged them with a nod of her head. She probably should have curtsied or bowed, but Roland still had her by the shoulders and didn't seem to want to let her go. "This is Sandor, partner to Darian" he motioned to a sparkling copper dragon, and then to the blue-green female at his side, "and this is his mate, Kelzy, partner to Gareth."

"Kelzy!" Lana looked to her mother for confirmation and was rewarded with her beaming smile and nodding head. "Lady Kelzy, my mother told us about you when we were just little girls. Mama said she used to bring you melons from her family's garden!"

Kelzy licked her chops with a twinkle in her eye. *And tasty they were too.*

A commotion from the main archway had them all looking over to see two twin black dragons being chased inside by a sparkling bright crystal dragon. She heard her new family's gasps with just a hint of pride. Roland was right about the stir Tor would cause, and she was so proud of him, she could burst. If there was one thing she'd done right in her life, he was it.

Roland released her as she moved to intercept her friend. Tor was playing a game of chasing the black dragons' tails and having a rollicking good time of it, from what she could see. Connor and Darius chuckled smokily as they led him to the center of the room, but when Tor saw her, he left off the game to toddle over to her on his growing back legs.

Lana! We had fun!

She reached up to stroke his head and neck, smiling at her closest friend in the whole world.

"I'm glad. They're good dragons." She smiled at the two brothers whom she well knew were more than just dragons. Darius winked back at her, a dragonish chuckle clouding the vented air above her head.

They're the best! They said I can play with their younger brother too, when he gets home from training. He's only a little bit older than me and we flew all around, and I showed them some of the tricks I use to get away from Salomar's crossbows. They said I can show the other dragons too!

"That's great, Tor. I think that will help them a lot. I have some people I want you to meet. Do you remember me telling you about my family? Sweetheart," she tried to break the news gently, unsure of how he might react, "Roland knew where my mother and sister were and he asked them to come here. They want to meet you."

Tor backed up, looking down into her face. *I'm really happy for you, Lana.* His voice was more hesitant than she ever remembered hearing. *Do you think Roland could find my mama too? 'Cause if you can't be my mama anymore, I'd like to have someone to love me.*

She will always be your mama, little one. Kelzy's large head loomed over them as she moved close, her wings outstretched to comfort. *I don't know how it happened, but the mother bond can never be broken among our kind. Don't fear, youngling, you have a big family now. I'm your grandmamma.*

Tor's sparkling diamond eyes looked up at the blue-green dragon with awe. *Grandmamma? I have a dragon grandmamma?*

And a grandpapa, an aunt and uncle too, Kelzy confirmed. Tor grew more excited as each of the dragons came forward to surround him in a circle of love. *We're Lana's family, and yours too. If you want us.* Kelzy shot him a sly, sideways look and the young Ice Dragon jumped with excitement.

Want you? Of course I do! Lana, this is great! His enthusiasm was contagious. He turned back to Kelzy and looked up at her earnestly. *Will you teach me dragon things? Lana feels like a dragon but she can't fly and flame and stuff. I had to figure that out on my own, though she tried to help.*

Kelzy reached out a sheltering wing, holding the dragonet to her side. *Of course we'll teach you all you should know, and you will show us what you've learned on your own. This way, we'll teach each other.*

Just that easily, Tor was back to his usual buoyant self. Kelzy was a special dragon, indeed, and in that moment, Lana's heart opened to the motherly dragon for the kindness she showed to Tor.

Lana, where's Roland? I want to tell him about my new family.

Lana looked to the man behind her. He sighed and stepped forward with a smile to face the giant dragonet.

Tor, do you know what a secret is?

Tor's head craned out from under Kelzy's wing, searching the room for Roland. *Of course I know that, Roland. Lana and I had to keep a lot of secrets before we got away from Salomar. I never let him know that I could flame or fly until we were ready to escape. Right, Lana? I kept those secrets good, like you told me. Where are you, Roland?*

The king stepped forward to stand before the dragon, motioning everyone else back. Only Lana remained at his side, just close enough to allow for his change.

"I'm here, Tor."

The dragonet's head pulled back, then leaned in to look him over carefully. He walked out from under Kelzy's wing to stand before Roland, eyeing him in some confusion.

Roland? The little voice was tentative, almost plaintive.

"Yes, son. I'm Roland. Watch and learn a secret you must keep among dragonkind."

So saying, Roland allowed the black mist to form and, within moments, became the black dragon that was half of his soul. Tor dropped back, stumbling on his feet to land on his tail. His diamond eyes were wide and awestruck.

You're like Lana, but even more! Dragon and human, he breathed, surprising the witnesses with his simple statement. *Before my mama left, when I was in the shell, she told me stories about your kind. You're wizard-breed!* Inexplicably, Tor dropped to his belly, cowering before Roland as if he were afraid. Lana dropped down to kneel at the side of his head, stroking him gently, offering comfort.

"Sweetheart, what is it?"

Wizard-breed are rulers of dragons. That's what Mama said. Must show respect.

Roland laughed kindly, shifting back to human form so he could bend down on the other side. "Respect, son, not complete subservience. Please get up off the floor. I wouldn't want anyone to walk on you. You make a rather lumpy carpet."

He chuckled as Tor cocked his head, watching him carefully. Slowly, the dragonet eased up from the floor, careful to keep his head down.

"Tor, look at me." Roland's voice was full of command. "I'm king of Draconia. Your mama was right. For generations, my family has ruled over dragons and people alike here, in peace, but we're not tyrants. You had fun playing with my brothers, didn't you?"

Brothers?

The two black dragons at the back of the room came forward, black mist rising as they walked, and within moments, two identical black-leather-clad young men walked in their tracks. Both had the same shining, peridot eyes and matching rakish grins as they stood on either side of their older brother, in front of Tor.

"I'm Darius," one said with a wink.

"And I'm Connor." He was a bit more solemn of the two. "We enjoyed flying with you, Tor. You've taught us a thing or two already."

"Roland, he flies like something out of legend. He's amazing!" Darius' enthusiasm was hard to miss.

Roland smiled, but there was more to tell the stunned dragonet. Changes were happening fast and furious.

"Tor," Roland lowered his voice, "I've asked Lana to be my mate. Do you understand what that means?"

Yes, his voice was small as he looked over at Lana, his eyes sad, *you'll live together and have babies.*

"Yes, Tor, but more than that. Lana will be my queen, and you'll be my son."

Your son? Hope blossomed in the baby dragon's eyes. *For real?*

Roland laughed. "Yes, for real, and for always. That means Darius and Connor, and my other brothers will be your uncles. You'll be part of the royal family Tor, and you'll be much loved."

Lana, is this true?

"It's true, baby. We both will have a big family now, with people and dragons to love us." She stroked his long neck. "What do you say? Should we stay here and try it out for a while?"

Tor's entire body shivered in excited delight. *I say we stay forever!*

Everybody laughed then and they milled around for a long time afterward getting to know each other. All were impressed by Tor, both by his size and by the size of his good-natured heart.

Lana found herself watching from the sidelines as everyone crowded around Tor, showering him with attention and the love he needed. This was a good place for him, surrounded by dragons and people who understood and loved dragons. Coming here had been the best thing for him, but she wasn't so sure about her own fate in this strange land.

She stood back, watching while Roland introduced everyone to Tor, already taking on the role of father. Tor looked up to him so much already, it was wonderful to think Tor would finally have a male role model in his life, especially a man such as Roland, who was everything good and worthy in a male of any species.

Lana was afraid, though, of what Roland would ask of her. She didn't know how to be queen of anything and she feared she would embarrass him before his people. Her doubt must have showed on her face because she became aware of a warm, motherly presence at her back. Turning, she found Kelzy there, staring down at her with a knowing look in her wise old eyes.

The blue-green dragon lowered her head to gaze closely at Lana. *You should not doubt yourself, Princess Alania. You'll be the best queen this land has seen in many generations. You understand dragons and you've seen the hard side of life. Too often in the past the men of the royal line have taken wives who were not their equals. With Roland and you begins the cycle of renewal. You two will restore the balance of dragons and humans in this land, giving hope to both races. Just your presence here has already begun a great stir among dragonkind. Word is already spreading about the half-dragon queen. Your mother and sister were reason enough to hope, but none foresaw that Roland would find you and mate you. We have hope now that the Mother has plans for our kind that go beyond merely existing and biding time until the Wizards' return.*

Lana gasped and Kelzy smiled in her inscrutable way. *What do you mean, the Wizards' return?*

Caught that, did you? You're as bright as your mama. That's good. Roland will need a clever woman at his side if the prophesied time comes to pass during his reign. The prophecy is kept sacred among the royal lines and we dragons. The Wizards did not all choose to leave this realm voluntarily, Lana. Some will try to return, or so the prophecy states. When that happens, we dragons will stand for humanity, to save them from Wizard tyranny. That's our purpose and that's why we did not leave this realm along with the Wizards when they fled. We are Guardians and we have an obligation to fulfill. Until that time, we rest here, among humans, led by a human who is also one of us, as the Mother asked of us.

Stars! I never realized. Lana turned over the startling possibilities in her mind. Wizards were reputed to be the most powerful beings to ever live. Only dragons had magic equal to that of the Wizards, though it was of a slightly different flavor. Without dragonkind, regular folk wouldn't stand a chance against even one Wizard, much less a contingent of them.

Had you been raised with your birthright, you would have known all of this from the beginning. You women of the House of Kent bring hope to dragonkind. For many generations now, the black dragons have been in decline. Fewer are born to each generation, and our enemies seek to destroy the lines completely, as we thought they had done with the line of Kent. Finding you, your sister and your mother again gives us hope that the line of black dragons will continue, and so continue the pact made so long ago. You will be a good queen to both humans and dragons, Alania. Never fear. Your love for Roland will see you through.

I do love him.

Can you imagine living without him in your life?

I can imagine it, she shuddered, *but it's not pretty.*

Then you should have no fear. Follow your heart. Be happy. Marry Roland and have babies for us to love, little girls to carry the magic and little boys to fly with.

You make it sound so easy.

It is easy, girl! Easy as love. If love leads, all else will follow.

Chapter Ten

"You know, I remember you, Lord Darian." Roland felt tension in the air as the two older knights waited to hear what he would say. It had been one of the hardest things for him to get used to as king, people hanging on his every word, but he knew these men listened so intently because they worried he might not accept a former Lord of Skithdron. He was happy he could set them at ease on that at least. "My father spoke highly of you."

Darian seemed to relax a little. "Your father was a great man, sire. I was sorry to hear of his death. Please accept my condolences, late though they are."

"Thank you, Lord Darian." Roland eyed both of the older knights. "Actually, I wanted to talk to you two for a number of reasons. First, I would congratulate you both on your recent marriage. If your Adora is anything like her daughter, you will never find a better woman for you, your dragons, your Lair or our land. Protect her well and cherish her."

Jared and Darian both nodded, but it was Jared who spoke. "The women of the House of Kent are special. Each has a heart of gold and the courage of a dragon."

Roland liked the compliment in Jared's eyes as he looked over at the three women across the room. Adora had her arms around her two daughters, their heads close together as they shared the stories of their lives.

"One of the other things I wanted to talk to you two about has to do with the governance of the Border Lair. Jared, I know you've been leading the Lair along with Lady Kelzy quite successfully to this point, but now Kelzy and Sandor are reunited through your mating with Adora and partnership with Darian, I'm officially recognizing you all as the elders of the Border Lair. I understand the women and children who live in the Lair already look to Adora for guidance. This will just formalize her role. Do you think she'll mind?"

Jared smiled. "She may object at first to having a formal title, but she's been adjusting well to the idea that our people look to her for leadership. She's a natural when it comes to organizing the Lair folk, though she won't admit it. She just has a hard time admitting she's royalty. She sees herself as an ordinary healer."

"With most extraordinary powers," Roland chuckled. "I understand. I know Lana feels much the same. Being raised in a simpler way of life has led our ladies to devalue their true worth, but it's our job to spoil them." The older men laughed at his candor.

Roland grew serious once more. "I do have one other subject I'd like to discuss. You've both done an amazing job on the border but I could use your expertise here as well. I'd like you to come to the palace every few weeks or so. Sir Jared," he turned to face the older knight, "you were Counselor to my father. I'm hoping you'll take up that role for me as well." He turned to the other knight. "And you, Sir Darian. Your counsel would also be greatly appreciated. Your intimate knowledge of King Lucan and what he's become could help us further defend our land and people, if you're willing to act as Counselor. I'd like Sandor and Kelzy to sit on the Dragon's Council as well. I need the four of you—your wisdom and knowledge—so I may rule wisely."

"For myself, I would be honored, sire." Darian made a polite bow, his blue eyes flashing.

Jared was somewhat more reserved. "I served your father, Roland. I'll serve you with the same loyalty. I'm honored you would ask."

Roland reached out to shake Jared's hand, pulling him in for a quick, manly hug. This man was like a father to him, now that his own father was gone, though age-wise Jared was closer to an older brother.

"You're family now, Jared," Roland pointed out. "The Mother of All certainly knew what She was doing. I'll also need your help keeping my younger brothers in line." The uncharacteristic roll of his eyes had Jared laughing outright and Darian smiled as well.

"We saw Nico briefly yesterday, but I suppose he's off again to parts unknown?" Jared's eyes narrowed and Roland knew the older man had full knowledge of the pivotal role Nico played in the kingdom.

Roland nodded. "He's doing some reconnaissance for me, but I expect him back in a few days."

A commotion erupted from the doorway to the huge hall and all eyes turned to watch a weary young messenger run in to kneel before the king.

"Sire, scouts report Salomar's army is massing across the northern border. General Jures sent this letter for you." The youth propped a scroll on his outspread fingers, offering it up to Roland, though his hand trembled.

Roland recognized the messenger as one of the youngsters from the Northern Lair. He took the letter and broke it open, skimming over the long message quickly before turning back to the boy.

"You're Benny, right? Lady Alis' youngest?"

The boy, barely in his teens, gulped. "Yes, sire."

"You'll find your Aunt Tilly in the stillroom at this time of day, I think. Do you know where it is?" The boy nodded eagerly. "Go to her. You'll be staying here at the palace until things are settled up north. Which dragon brought you?"

"Rena, sire. She was too shy to come inside. She's waiting in the hallway."

Roland had to hide his chuckle. The little dragonet was just a baby and very shy, but quite a charmer already. "You did well, young Benny. Thank you for your speedy service."

He watched the youth scamper off before turning to the collection of knights, ladies and dragons, now silent in the big room. He realized suddenly this huge group was his family. He'd always had his brothers, of course, but for many years now, there were precious few people he could claim as kin. Tor was doing an odd little dance of impatience as he shuffled in place.

"You want to see your friend Rena, don't you?" he asked softly as Tor nodded and smoked in eager agreement. "All right, but I want you both to stay within sight of my brothers at all times, agreed?" He nodded to Darius and Connor, and both of them walked out after a bounding Tor, their mission clear to keep the baby dragons safe in their care.

"Well, it seems I'll need your counsel even sooner than I'd thought." Roland sighed as Darian and Jared moved forward, Gareth and Lars following only a step behind. "Lana," he looked around the wall of knights to see his betrothed, "we could use your insight. You know best what Salomar will bring against us."

Brushing at her skirt self-consciously, Lana stepped forward to Roland's side, within the circle of men. Roland tucked her close, drawing comfort from her presence. He stood at the center of the knights. The older dragons gathered round as he read through the long letter from Jures, reading portions aloud so all could hear what was going on up north.

When he finished, he looked up at the grim faces all around. The news was not good.

"Sire," a soft voice came from behind him. He turned to find Lana's mother and sister hadn't been idle. They'd moved chairs from the walls and apparently found a table from somewhere.

Roland took Adora's hand, kissing it respectfully. "You are a treasure, milady. Thank you for thinking of our comfort." She blushed prettily and Roland saw immediately where his Lana got her grace. She was indeed her mother's daughter.

Leading the way, he pulled out a chair and seated Lana first, then took the chair at her side. He was only mildly surprised when the other ladies took seats between their knights. The dragons gathered round the table, making themselves as comfortable as possible in the large space.

Thus, they sat for over an hour, going through each paragraph and sentence of Jures' detailed letter, strategizing and surmising what might come next. Lana's insight was invaluable. She was able to tell them all she knew about Salomar's troops, their specialties, their strengths and weaknesses. Roland made special note of how her knowledge meshed with the observations made by Jures and his scouts. One thing was certain, the northern border was in dire straits.

Roland stood in frustration, pacing behind the table as those around it watched him warily. The dragon within him wanted to roar and flame, but the man needed to be in control for just a little longer.

146

He had decisions to make and they would affect great numbers of people. The responsibility was daunting, but it was one he'd gotten used to over the years.

"I'm going to the Northern Lair. Tonight."

"Sire, I don't think that's wise." It was Gareth who spoke. The older knights just regarded Roland with their mouths held in tight, grim lines. "You're too important to the kingdom."

"Thank you for that, Gareth, but I must go. I'll disperse my brothers to the other Lairs in case this is some kind of feint. The youngest of my brothers will stay here at the palace for safety. The line of Draneth will be preserved." His focus turned to Lana, resigned to what must be. "But Lana and Tor must go north with me. They need to be at the Northern Lair to share what they know about Salomar's men. They're our only experts on what's coming our way and I'll be damned if I let either one of them go anywhere without me. As it is, if I had any choice, I wouldn't put them within fifty leagues of the battle, but there's no other way."

Roland felt Lana come to his side, her little hand gripping his reassuringly. "You couldn't keep me away, Roland." Her voice was low but he knew it carried to all present. "This is one of the few things I can truly help you with. I don't want Tor in danger either, but we need to do this. Salomar hurt us both too much. Tor and I already talked this over. We don't want to see Salomar hurt anyone else if we can help prevent it."

He tugged her into his arms, hugging her tight. His Lana had more courage than fifty knights.

"I understand," he said softly, his eyes grim. "That's why we're all going together to the Northern Lair, but when it comes time for battle, you and Tor are staying in the Lair. I won't have either of you put directly in harm's way."

She nodded solemnly up at him and he kissed her hard and fast, sealing the deal.

They flew far that night, pausing a few times to let Tor rest, but by morning they were at the Northern Lair. Word spread quickly of their arrival. Within moments, Hal and Jures were there to greet them, but Hal's usual teasing smile was missing. The man had become all warrior now that a serious threat faced his family and the people and dragons of his Lair.

"Welcome back, sire. Thank you for coming." Jures' respect was evident in his formal tone as they started walking toward the inner recesses of the Lair.

"What news?" Roland asked as they walked.

"The bulk of the enemy army has settled on a plain not far distant where the river bends and narrows." Hal spoke from the other side as they continued walking urgently down the wide hall. Lana kept close at Roland's side while Tor followed behind.

"I know the place," Roland said tersely, nodding.

"We believe they will try to cross there."

"It makes sense," Roland mused, "though why so obvious? Head-on fighting is not Salomar's style. He's more devious than that. What deeper game is he playing, I wonder?"

"Perhaps he thinks his new weapons will be surprise enough to defeat you," Lana said, noting all the men were listening attentively. "Or even if they're not a surprise, perhaps he thinks they'll cause real trouble for you and your dragons."

"Could be." Roland escorted her into a large chamber where a group of dragons and knights already waited, some of whom she knew from her earlier visit to the Northern Lair. The humans stood as

Roland entered, making signs of respect, and the dragons bowed their heads slightly as he passed.

This was the war council, the meeting clearly in progress. Roland seated Lana at his side, taking charge of the meeting and going through what they knew and what they surmised from scouts and reconnaissance. Tor walked over to the other dragons, happy enough to settle between Tilden and Rue, who greeted him with soft snuffles and touches of their sinuous necks to his. Roland called on Tor's expertise as they discussed Salomar's weapons in much greater detail than they ever had before.

Lana, Tor and Roland stayed closeted with the war council of the Northern Lair for most of the day. Roland seemed to have energy to spare, but Tor and Lana started to feel the strain of the long night's flight. Roland, apparently sensing their fatigue, called a recess and took the time to escort them to the suite of rooms they'd used before. He settled them both before going off with the knights for more discussions of strategy and preparations for war. Lana wanted to stay with him, but she was just too tired. The momentous events of the past few days had finally caught up with her. She fell asleep between one thought and the next.

When she woke a few hours later, Tor was still curled in his warm wallow, but there was a strange, small black dragon at his side. Cocking her head in question, Lana knew the black dragon had to be one of the royal princes, but from his size, he had to be quite young and to her knowledge, she had not yet met this one.

She had only a moment to consider it, for Roland walked in as she was about to go looking for him. He stopped dead in his tracks as he caught sight of the little black dragon, his eyes flashing fury.

"William!" he thundered, causing both sleepy dragons to blink blearily.

The little black scampered back from Roland's obvious wrath. He hopped out of the wallow and changed to human form. Lana realized he was just a boy, maybe a teen at best.

"What do you think you're doing here?"

"I wanted to meet your girlfriend and the Ice Dragon."

Roland advanced on the boy, anger in every movement. "We're about to go to war here, Wil. This is no place for you."

"You're here. And so are they." He looked accusingly at both Lana and Tor before turning back to his brother, courage in every line of his young body. "I don't see why I shouldn't be here too."

"It's too dangerous. Believe me," Roland ran an exasperated hand through his hair, "if not for the knowledge they have about the Northern army, they'd be safely back at the castle, where *you're* supposed to be. Blast it, Wil! I don't want any of you here. It's too dangerous."

"Sire!" Jures ran into the room. "Salomar's forces are advancing across the Arundelle." Lana knew that was the name of the river marking the boundary between the two lands. The battle was beginning.

Roland's eyes hardened. "I'll be right there. Form up the ranks." He turned to Lana and strode forward to take her into his arms. Delivering a quick, hard kiss, he let her go. "I want you to stay here, sweetheart." He began moving into the short hall leading to the ledge and she followed.

"But—" Suddenly she needed to be at his side, fighting with him. She got the feeling if she wasn't with him, she would never see him again. The idea made her shiver with fear. "Let us go with you! Tor and I can help. We've fought them before."

Roland stopped in his tracks to pull her against his hard body. "I can't." He crushed her to his chest and she felt the tremble of raw emotion in his powerful arms. "I can't put you in danger, my love. Neither you, nor Tor." He kissed her roughly, the need to possess seeming to overcome his more civilized human side for a moment. She didn't mind at all as something wild inside her own soul answered his urgency. "I'm leaving William to watch over you." He said it loudly, looking over her shoulder to the boy who trailed after them. "Promise me you'll stay with him and keep each other safe." He refocused on her, pitching his voice lower. "Please. If you go out with Tor, I'll have no way of keeping William behind and he's too young for what we'll be facing. If I give him the mission of protecting you and Tor, he'll stay. I need to know you're safe—all three of you."

He was pleading with her and she could not refuse him. The emotion in his green eyes was so deep, so genuine, she knew she couldn't make his burden even heavier by insisting. Slowly, she nodded, praying her sudden feelings of dread were all wrong.

"I'd rather be out there helping, but I'll keep William safe for you."

"That is help, my love. That boy would be in the thick of it without some honorable reason to keep him here. He's too brash, too young, and I don't want him hurt."

She nodded against his chest. "I'll keep him safe."

"And yourself and Tor." He raised her chin with one gentle hand. "I love you more than life, Lana. I couldn't take it if you were hurt. It's my weakness, not any of yours. Please understand that. I know you're a capable woman. I know you fought and evaded Salomar's soldiers for years before I ever knew you, but I can't help the need I have to know that you're safe. Thank you for humoring me." His gentle smile warmed her heart.

"I love you too, Roland."

He kissed her long and deep then, lighting a fire they didn't have time to quench. When he pulled away, he held her gaze for long moments before finally stepping back to transform. A moment later, the man was gone in a swirl of black mist and the dragon stood in his place, breathing warm air over her. His long tongue licked out and wrapped around her neck briefly in a caress before brushing across her cheek.

Stay safe, my love, and keep William and Tor by your side. I don't trust either of those two young scamps to stay put unless they are within your sight.

"I'll keep them close. And safe."

Then I can ask no more. You put my mind at ease. Stay here and try not to worry. I'll be back as soon as I can. Never forget that I love you with all my heart, Alania.

"I love you too, Roland." A tear trickled down her face as she walked with him out to the landing ledge where dragons and knights were grouped in number, ready for flight. He took his place at the head of them and launched, leaving her behind with a trumpeting roar.

Almost immediately after the last of the fighting pairs were gone, she felt Tor's large body nestle up against her side. He was a little scared, judging from the slight tremor in his forelegs, so she put her arms around him.

"It will be all right, Tor."

They stood there for a moment before she became aware of the smaller black dragon watching them. She moved back from Tor and regarded her other charge. William. Somewhere along the line he'd changed to dragon form and followed Tor.

I'm to stay and guard you two. Wil didn't sound all that happy about his assignment, but willing to carry out his duty nonetheless.

Lana smiled and walked up to him. "Thank you, Prince William. Tor and I are glad of your protection." Her thoughts turned grave, though she tried to keep a brave face for the youngsters. "Though like you, we'd rather be out there helping."

The black's head tilted to the side. *If we go up top we can probably watch most of the battle.*

Can we? Tor piped in, moving closer.

"Is it safe?"

William snorted smokily. *We're miles away. It's safe. There's a lookout position up there. Our sentries use it all the time.*

A few minutes later, Lana found herself with Tor and a now-human William near the lookout post at the top of the peak into which the Lair was built. One young man had been left behind to act as sentry, but he didn't object to their company and even loaned Lana an extra viewing lens they used to see far distances. After he showed her how to use it, she could see a great deal of the action as the battle was launched. She couldn't see the knights' faces, but she recognized individual dragons and Roland was easily identifiable, leading them.

She watched as he employed the tactics Tor had shown them against Salomar's weapons and seemingly endless army. There were so many soldiers! Where had they all come from? She hadn't suspected Salomar commanded so many men.

Lana recognized the big, rolling machines they used to fire diamond-bladed bolts into the sky and cheered when each of their shots missed their marks. The dragons were using what Tor had learned and passed on to avoid the potentially deadly bolts. A few dragons were caught by some of the other traps, but none were hurt too badly. Lana felt her palms itch with power, needing to heal them, but knew she would get her chance to help when they came back to the Lair. For now, she could only watch from afar as the battle progressed.

She followed Roland most of all, watching his skill in the sky with joy. He performed acrobatic feats many of the other dragons could not due to their greater size and bulk. He also didn't have to worry about a rider on his back and achieved angles much steeper than the other dragons who had their knights to consider. He was graceful and fierce, flaming brighter and flying faster than any of the dragons, though she thought privately Tor might give him a run for his money when he was fully grown.

She loved them both so much. She kept one hand on Tor's sinuous neck, the other on the lens through which she watched the action. Tor and Wil saw well enough with their sharp dragon eyes, but she needed the lens, limited by her human body. Even so, she was the first to see disaster when it struck.

"Roland!" She screamed as she saw the black dragon fall, tears whipping down her face as something inside her stirred to life. Something wild. Something untamed. "Roland!"

She fell to her knees on the ground as the ache in her heart turned to molten fire, spreading outward to her limbs. She hurt all over and realized something was terribly wrong. Not just with Roland, but with her own body. She looked up to see Tor winging away at full speed toward the battle and she knew her baby was heading out to try to save Roland. Without her. He was going into danger without her!

Anger stirred. Anger, determination and a soul-blinding fury of flame that came from deep within. She caught movement at her side and watched the black mist envelop William as he changed.

But no, the black mist wasn't around William, it was around her own body.

"What's happening to me?"

"Stars above!" William whispered in awe as he backed away from her. "You're changing, Lana. Don't fight it! Let the change take you. Fighting will only make it hurt more this first time."

His words followed her into the mist as all light faded from view, only to come back in startling clarity a moment later as she came back to herself. Her eyesight was a thousand times sharper. At first she thought she must still be looking through the borrowed lens but as she blinked, she realized two things—first, that she was looking through her own eyes, not the lens, and second, her eyes were huge!

She was no longer human. Lana tried to move her head to look down at herself, but everything felt foreign and strange. She was high above where her body should be, looking down on a…a…black dragon. A female black dragon.

Sweet Mother! I'm a dragon.

Wil barked in startled laughter as his eyes widened. *You've never changed before, have you?*

I didn't know I could. Before I met Roland, I didn't know anyone could. Oh, no, Roland!

She turned her ponderous head and realized she could easily see the action so far away now without the lens. Her dragon eyes were much more acute. Her heart reached out to her fallen lover and she knew he was unconscious…or worse. Roland wasn't moving at all. He was definitely down and within range of Salomar's men, vulnerable on the ground. Tor was nearing him at a fast pace but he would need help and all the other knights and dragons seemed to be engaged. She saw a haze over the battlefield. It was an unnatural, ghostly blue glow springing up like a barrier between the dragons and knights and where Roland lay on the ground. She saw how it prevented anyone from getting close enough to help him. It was evil magic, she knew it in her bones.

She unfurled her wings in agitation and flapped, surprising herself when she lifted off the ground.

Stars! Can I fly?

I don't see why not.

Wil's calm voice steadied her. She could do this. She'd helped Tor learn to fly, after all. She knew how he did it in theory, and Roland needed help. As did Tor. He was big and brave, but he couldn't stand alone against that many armed men and still manage to help Roland. They needed her.

I'm going to help them. She flapped a few more times and took a running leap off the high ledge, surprised when she started to soar rather than plummet. She flapped her wings and started to get used to the rhythm of flying, the way she'd seen Tor do so often. She felt a presence at her side and looked over to see the smaller black dragon alongside, watching her.

You're not going without me. I promised Roland I'd look after you.

I promised him the same thing about you. If you get hurt, he'll never forgive me.

I could say the same, sister. Wil chuckled softly, streaming smoke out behind him as they ate up the distance between the Lair and the battlefield. *I don't know what he's going to say when he sees you. To my knowledge, there hasn't been a female black dragon in centuries.*

She fumbled in the air a bit as she got used to the beat of her wings. She was small and fast, maybe even faster than Tor, she realized as she caught up to him quicker than she thought she would. He was running below the weapons fire, evading the bolts and shards sent at him from the ground and just skimming the tops of the swordsmen's reach as he made his way to Roland.

Lana knew she'd have to follow that same deadly path if she was going to help. William too, but at least the young prince had more flying and fighting training than she did.

Damn, he's good, Wil commented as he watched Tor's dangerous path. *They're going to be watching for us to do the same. Can you flame?*

The thought shocked her. *I don't know.*

Now would be a good time to find out. Take a deep breath and then let it out through your mouth. The flame should engage at the back of your throat. It'll feel warm and a little ticklish. Aim with your neck. Point your head where you want it to go and narrow your mouth to narrow the stream. It'll shoot farther that way.

Lana tried to do what he said, shocking herself almost to the point of falling out of the sky when a small belch of flame shot past her claws. Immediately, she began beating her wings again. This body felt awkward, to say the least, but she was getting the hang of things. Having spent so much time with Tor helped, though she had a whole new appreciation for the things he'd learned all on his own now that she was doing them herself.

Good. Just don't forget to fly! Wil cheered her on as they neared the battle line. Tor was on the ground now, flaming and flaring his wings, keeping the soldiers off Roland. *Keep your belly to them and do your best to shield your joints where the scales meet. A lucky shot between the scales could bring you down all too easily and then Roland will kill me for sure.*

Wil's attempt at humor made her realize just how risky this entire maneuver was, but without their help, Roland would die. The enemy was deliberately keeping the knights and dragons away from Roland, and though they were trying desperately to fight through, the enemy was all too clever.

She had no more time to think as they swooped over the enemy soldiers. Wil flamed as he went. Tor had not thought to do so, relying on his speed and flying skills to get him through. Wil's flames took a few of the soldiers by surprise before the rest brought up their shields. The shields helped protect them from the worst of the fire, but they also prevented the soldiers from firing any more bolts at the racing streaks of the black dragons.

Now, Lana! Now! Flame now!

Wil's urgent voice broke through to her and she breathed as he'd told her to do, amazed when the fire leapt out of her newly formed jaw to the ground and soldiers below. She heard a man scream as she burned him but she couldn't spare him much sympathy. These men were trying to kill her! Worse, they were trying to kill Roland and Tor. She would do anything to protect them. Anything.

A few more harrowing moments and they were through the army, dropping through Tor's flame to Roland's side. Wil took up a position back to back with Tor and taught the younger dragon how to lay down a wall of flame encircling the two blacks in the middle.

Lana fell out of the sky with little grace, nearly landing right on Roland as she fell, but she caught herself just in time. Without even thinking, she transformed to human and laid her healing hands on Roland's severe injuries. He was so close to death!

Calling on all the ancient power within her, she closed his wounds, sealing the deadly gashes from the inside out. The power came from them both, feeding upon each other, strengthening her ability to heal without tiring her. Never before had she done so extensive a healing without falling unconscious, but this time, she felt enervated. Roland opened his eyes, blinking at her.

Lana? How did you get here?

"Not now, my love." She kissed him gently but urgently on the cheek. "Can you fly?"

I think so. He shook himself as he stood, appearing more than a bit disoriented. He'd been close to death only moments before having taken a bone-crushing fall from the sky.

Lana stood also, gasping as she saw the woman who walked with impunity, right through the dragons' flames to peer at her.

It was Loralie, the North Witch. Lana stood in front of Roland, facing the other woman down.

"Stay back, witch. You cannot have him."

Loralie smiled coyly and walked closer. "Be at ease, little one. I'm here for my own reasons." She held Lana's gaze. "To help. To keep Salomar from using me any further in this battle."

"I don't believe you."

The witch shrugged. "Believe me or not, I'm glad to see you and the dragonet are doing well." The woman calmly took a blade from her waist, and though Lana started, she made no move to come closer to any of them. No, the witch turned the blade on herself, slicing her clothing in three long gashes, also slicing into the pale skin beneath. When she was done, the wounds looked almost exactly like the marks made by a dragon's slashing talons. The witch threw the blade to her and Lana caught it reflexively.

"A gift. Take it with you or he'll know what I've done. Go, little one. Take them and go. Please."

It was the plea in her voice that got Lana moving. For whatever reason, the witch was letting them go. If it were some kind of trick, she would kill the woman outright, but for now, she would trust...a little. Clutching the witch's blade carefully between her fingers, Lana stood back and called on the fire she had only just found awakened within her and sought the change.

The black mist enveloped her and it was much less painful this time. No, this time, it was wondrous. She felt herself change in the blink of an eye, and a moment later, she stood next to Roland, smaller than he, but just as dragonish.

Lana? he questioned.

Yes, my love. She stumbled a bit on her new legs, touching noses with him for a swift moment. *We'll talk about it when we get back. Can you fly now?*

Yes!

Roland breathed deeply, turning to help the younger dragons with their circle of flame so they could clear a path for their launch. Lana watched the witch carefully, but the woman was smiling.

"So you've discovered your birthright. Congratulations, Alania. You've done better than I ever expected."

As if you care for my welfare. Lana thought at the witch, knowing the other woman could probably pick up on dragonish speech.

"I have always kept an eye on you, Lana. When you were stolen, I chose to follow you rather than your sister. I knew you would be the one for him." Her eyes moved to the black dragon at her back. Roland.

Do you know where Riki is?

The witch smiled as she lay down on the ground at an odd angle, as if wounded. "Your sister is in the east, serving the mad king. I protected her from him as best I could, but I wasn't able to do much. The Prince of Spies will find her. I have foreseen it."

Time to go. Roland was still clearly dazed and his eyes had trouble focusing.

160

Lana looked down one last time at the witch. *I feel like I should thank you, but I don't understand why. You tried so many times to hurt Tor and me.*

"You may understand in time. For now, let us part as enemies. It's safer that way for all concerned."

At Roland's direction, Tor took off first with Wil right behind, then it was Lana's turn and Roland took up the rear by only a few seconds. Within moments, the four were winging their way back to their side of the battle. They flamed a path back to the lead pair, Tilden and Rue, with Hal and Jures on their backs.

Sire! Thank the Mother! We've been blocked at every angle. They came prepared to take you down.

Rest easy, Hal. I see that now. That was Salomar's deeper game. Not your fault. Regroup and go after the machines. They're made of wood under the hide shielding. Concentrated flame should torch them.

Aye, we'll torch the lot of them.

Hal had murder in his eyes as he and the dragon peeled away, Jures following close behind to carry out the king's orders.

Roland, you need to rest.

Lana? His sparkling green eyes turned on her. *How in the world did you shift?*

I have no idea. I saw you go down, she hiccupped and smoke came out of her dragonish mouth, startling her so much she faltered before picking up the rhythm of her wings again, *and Tor took off after you without me. I had to get to you. And it just happened.*

You should've seen it, Rol! Wil's voice was eager in their minds as he dropped back beside them now that they were out of danger. *She was great her first time out. A natural.*

Tor raced ahead for the cliff top, roaring for her as he landed.

Lana! Lana! Where are you?

Lana was still incredibly awkward when she tried to land, but Roland coached her, landing first and catching her hurtling body with his larger one when she would have overshot her landing. Tor was pacing up and down now, looking for her.

I'm here, Tor, she finally answered him. She had no idea how he would take this new change. She stood on her shaky dragon legs and walked over to the large baby dragon she had raised. He was so much bigger than she was, even now.

Lana? Tor's voice was hesitant.

Yes, baby. It's me.

Lana! You are *my mommy!*

Chapter Eleven

Lana found it harder to change back now that the stress of the moment was gone. She had to make her way back down to the Lair in dragon form. Roland stayed on one side, Tor frolicking along on the other, each helping her maneuver her awkward dragon body toward a private suite with a large, heated sand pit.

Tor jumped in first, rolling around and polishing his gleaming scales while the warm sand soothed his tired muscles.

Ready to join him? I can assure you, there's nothing better than warm sand on your scales after a hard flight.

Come on, Lana! Tor called, showering sand everywhere. Wil jumped in next to the dragonet and splashed sand at him playfully. A little game ensued, Tor giggling smokily as he played with Wil in dragon form.

You're a dragon now, my love. You'll enjoy this. I promise.

But—

Trust me, Lana.

With a firm shove of his foreleg, he pushed her over the edge of the pit and into the warm sand. She tumbled a bit, flustered by the sudden movement and more awkward than ever on her new limbs, but the warmth of the sand penetrated her new thickly-scaled skin.

Oh, this feels really wonderful.

Roland chuckled as he joined her, smoke rising through the air to the vented, domed roof of the suite. He tucked his wings back behind him and grappled her in close to his larger dragon body with strong forelegs.

What did I tell you? Now let's play.

Play?

She didn't get to ask anything further as he rolled with her into the warm sand, twining his sinuous neck with hers. She would have screamed, but it came out more like a trumpeting call from her dragon mouth. She accidentally let out some flame, too, but his dragon hide was impervious to it, thank the Mother. She had a hard time controlling her body in this form, but she was learning as she went.

Roland pinned her beneath his massive body, aligning them in this new form just as easily as he did when they were human. Sand showered over them and she heard dragonish snorts of laughter from the two younger males who were using their wingtips to shovel warm sand over them both.

Roland looked into her eyes, his wings sheltering her as she lay beneath him. Her own wings were tucked up uncomfortably behind her and she shifted to try to ease them. Roland let up immediately.

Stretch your wings, my love. Rub them in the warm, healing sand.

Oh, that feels good. Lana stretched beneath him, getting just a bit more comfortable in her new body, but she was more than ready to be human again. *Roland, why can't I change back? It was easy before. Why is it so difficult this time?*

The more you think about changing, the harder it becomes. The first times you changed, you were probably too preoccupied with what was going on around you to worry about shifting. You just did it, right?

She nodded her head, still smaller than him, but she felt herself to be huge compared to her human form. It was ungainly and hard to deal with, especially on land.

So you think I'm over-thinking it?

I'd say that's a definite possibility. Hence, the sand bath. Nothing relaxes a dragon better than a good roll in a warm wallow. I think once you're relaxed, the shift will happen of its own volition.

I hope you're right.

Roland moved away, allowing her room as Tor's curious head bobbed between them.

Isn't this great, Lana? You're a dragon too. We can play tag in the sky now, once you learn to fly better.

Lana stretched her wings out and around the dragonet, hugging all of him for once in his life. He's always been so much bigger than her. He still was, but at least for now, while he was still a baby, she could get her wings around him.

You'll have to teach me all about being a dragon, Tor.

Roland will help. He's teaching me new stuff all the time. Tor snuggled in close to her, burrowing into her embrace. *I'm so happy here, Lana, but why didn't you ever change before?*

I didn't know I could.

That's all right. I always knew you were a dragon inside.

She thought back on all the times Tor had said as much and wondered. Somehow he had recognized the dragon in her, even when she had no idea of her origins. Tor snuggled close a few moments longer, then wiggled free to play with Wil on the other side of the huge wallow. Roland lay next to her, apparently content in the warm sand.

You ready to try that shift now?

Lana sighed heavily, startled by the smoke rising out of her mouth. *Ready as I'll ever be, I guess.*

Roland reached out with just the tip of his long tail, trailing it lightly down her side as he talked her gently through the change. It took her long minutes to relax to the point where his voice in her mind lulled her. Following his lead, she shifted back to her human form, shocked when she found herself entirely naked.

She squeaked and tried to cover herself. Luckily Wil was off on the other side of the room, playing with Tor and couldn't see her predicament.

"What happened to my clothes?"

Roland laughed softly and shrugged out of his leather tunic, dropping it over her shoulders. Luckily, his big shirt hung well past her hips, almost like a dress.

"The dragon magic allows our clothing to come with us—or leave us—in the change. You have to think of the clothes on you while you change and they'll be there when you come back. I can't explain it any better than that. It'll take practice, but you'll get there in time." He stroked her hair as they lay back in the warm, enveloping sand. "I can hardly believe the Mother has blessed me so, to give me the perfect mate."

She snorted self-consciously. "I'm far from perfect."

He kissed her so gently, the look in his darkening eyes melting her heart.

"You're perfect for me, my love." His hand stroked down her side to settle at her waist while he leaned over her on their warm bed of sand. "I knew before that I was a lucky, blessed man, but now…" His hand slid over her arm to grasp her fingers, squeezing tight as he held her gaze. "Now that you've found the dragon within you, you are my perfect match in every possible way. Think of the possibilities, Lana. We can soar to the stars now. Together."

Her breath caught at the image that popped into her mind. From his? She wasn't sure, but she saw two black dragons twined around each other as they shot toward the sun.

"A mating flight?" Her voice was breathless with the idea. Breathless and hot.

His smile was sexy and low. "There hasn't been a royal mating flight in centuries. We'll be the first in all that time so perfectly matched that we can make love in both forms. I've heard it's amazing."

"And dangerous! We could plummet to the ground if we don't break apart in time."

He chuckled and kissed her nose. "I'll trust you to keep us on track, little one. Besides, that's part of the thrill. Ecstasy in freefall. My dragon side tells me there's nothing to compare it with in human terms."

She found herself stroking his strong shoulders, thinking through the tantalizing possibilities.

"I'd have to fly better than I do right now."

"I'll practice with you every day." He brought her little hand to his lips and kissed her palm, the light in his eyes dancing with excitement and joy. She felt herself responding to his eagerness.

"I'd like that."

CRCRCR

The battle ended with the Northern army in full retreat. Once the witch took herself out of the battle—for whatever reason she'd done that—the dragons were better able to maneuver. Somehow her magic had kept them blocked. They all reported the strange phenomenon as they returned, confused by the magic used against them. The only dragons who hadn't felt Loralie's influence were the three blacks and Tor. They'd flown right through the field that was off limits to the others, as if nothing blocked their path.

And perhaps nothing did.

Whether it was their own magic, being slightly different from that of the other dragons, or some trick of the North Witch, neither the blacks nor the Ice Dragon felt the effects of her spell. It was clear to all that Roland had been the target of the entire attack, and the Witch was instrumental in all that had occurred—for good and ill.

Loralie's odd actions were the topic of much conjecture among the king, his family and his advisors for days after the battle, but none could fathom exactly what the woman had up her sleeve. Whether she was truly an enemy or a hidden ally remained to be seen.

Loralie's dagger was also the topic of much conversation. After flying back to the Lair, Lana gave the knife to Roland and he passed it on to a knight named Branden who had a flair for history and knowledge of edged weapons. Branden said at first glance the dagger was a rare piece indeed, but he would consult with experts to learn what he could of its origins and report back. Lana was just glad to have the thing out of her sight. She didn't want to think about Loralie anymore. At least not right now.

Lana used her healing skills to patch up the injured dragons, only extending the legend she seemed to be building, giving of her own energy to heal the dragons of the Northern Lair. The dragons talked among themselves about her, the gorgeous and loving baby Ice Dragon who was her son, her amazing healing gift, and the fact that a mysterious third black dragon had been spotted from afar during the heat of the battle.

No one knew for certain just where that third black dragon had come from, racing in to save the king, flying in odd fits and starts. The dragons and knights spent their idle time trying to account for the various princes. Some suggested it might have been Prince Nico. Only he would have the nerve to dart in, save the day, then leave without a trace. It was just the sort of practical joke he would enjoy. But others said not.

Roland was physically well after the severe beating he'd taken during the battle, thanks to Lana's healing skills, but he took her advice and stayed on at the Northern Lair to both rest up and to receive scouting reports about the remainder of Salomar's army. He didn't think they'd heard the last of Salomar, and until that situation was resolved, he would keep a close eye on the northern border.

Each day Roland and Lana took a short trip to a quiet area where she practiced shifting and flying. She left the Lair on Tor's back, flying with Tor and Roland as they taught her how to be a dragon, then shifting back to arrive back in the Lair in human form with none the wiser.

"You know, they're going to find out sooner or later. Jures tells me they're all scratching their heads trying to figure out who that third black dragon was." Roland stroked her arm as they walked back to the suite they were using while they stayed at the Northern Lair. Tor had stayed outside to play with some of the younger dragons while the sun was high.

"I fly so badly." Her voice sounded so dejected, it touched his heart. "I'm embarrassed for them to see me until I can at least walk in dragon form without tripping over my tail."

"That's not true, sweetling. You're getting better every day." He put his arm around her as they stepped into the suite. "And the real proof is in what you did in battle. Having never flown before, you followed Tor's path—a feat for any dragon—and saved my life. No one will mind that you're still a little unsteady on your talons. Believe me."

They entered the open archway only to find two startled black dragons there before them. It was the older set of twins, Trey and Collin, who must have only just arrived from the deep south. In a swirl of black mist, they transformed to two tall, muscular, leather-clad warriors with identical stunning green eyes and dark blonde hair.

"Ah, the mystery is solved." Trey said with a friendly grin as he reached to grip his brother's hand in greeting. The other twin followed suit, both turning to look over the woman at Roland's side with interest flashing in their eyes. "The Lair is in an uproar trying to figure out who swooped in to save the day, Rol. We only just got here and they've already questioned us both, separately and together."

Roland hugged Lana close to his side. He felt her discomfort in the tightening of her shoulders, but she was a brave woman. She wouldn't let them see her nerves.

"This is Lana, my intended bride, and yes, she can shift."

Trey whistled between his teeth while Collin watched her quietly, clearly stunned.

"The first female black dragon in centuries." Awe resonated through Collin's deep voice as he looked down at Lana. "And she'll be your queen?" His eyes moved to Roland, admiration in their depths. "Congratulations to you both."

"Welcome to the family, sister."

Trey smiled broadly and took her hand, tugging her out of Roland's embrace. With a devilish twinkle, he hugged her close, loosing her only to pass her off to Collin for a similar embrace. Lana smiled and laughed at the familiar way his mischievous brothers handled her, and Roland's heart filled with joy at how well she fit in with his family. She would be the perfect queen, the perfect mate, his perfect love for the rest of their days. The Mother of All had truly blessed him when She'd sent him Lana and young Tor. He loved them both, deeply and true.

CRCRCR

Roland continued to teach Lana how to fly over the next few days. Trey and Collin remained close, flying out with the reconnaissance patrols to see what the remnants of the Northern army were doing. So far, they remained quiet in the foothills, neither retreating, nor advancing. Roland felt an itch between his shoulders warning him something was brewing up there.

Salomar wasn't done yet and they'd have to be on the lookout for renewed attack. For the time being, he decided to stay in the Northern Lair, sending Wil back to the palace both to keep him safe and as a messenger. Some messages were too important to entrust to anyone but family.

Through Wil, Roland dispatched his brother Nico out to the east to see what Skithdron was up to while he dealt with Salomar. Nico was his right hand, his eyes and ears in foreign lands. Prince Nico, the

Prince of Spies, would safeguard the east while Roland was preoccupied with the clear and present threat in the north.

Right now, it was a waiting game, but Roland knew something would have to give soon. Until then, he would keep his eyes and ears open and keep his eldest twin brothers near in case there was trouble. Both were proven warriors, only a few years younger than himself. They were good men to have at your back in a fight and he would trust not only his own safety, but that of his betrothed to their care.

With Wil safely back at the castle, Roland found a little time alone each day with Tor and Lana to continue her flying lessons. They'd found an idyllic little glade in which to practice her moves and she was getting a little steadier every time she flew, though she often over-thought her movements and ended up flailing awkwardly. She was at her best when she just moved without thinking and Roland tried his best to get her into that zone whenever possible.

That morning, Roland and Tor, with Lana on the dragonet's back, landed in their secret glade and all hell broke loose. Diamond-bladed arrows shot out at them from the surrounding trees, and Roland knew he had flown into an ambush, regardless of the fact he'd had patrols out scouting the area before he and Tor ever left the Lair.

Trey! Collin! We need you now!

Roland called to his brothers and trumpeted for help as he threw himself in front of Tor. The baby dragon was fast, but he'd already taken one hit to his foreleg from a lucky arrow as Lana scrambled off his back.

Roland flamed the trees, catching one of the archers, judging by the yelp of pain that followed, but the others were behind rock or otherwise protected. Using his powerful tail, Roland cut a swath through the vegetation, taking out any cover the villains might have. It was a small force, but dangerous enough with their extra sharp weapons.

If the dragons took to the air, all the most tender parts of their hides and delicate wings would be exposed. It was too risky. They had to hold on until help arrived. Roland's anger blossomed as the smelly Northerners threatened his family. With anger in every movement, he stalked the greasy men, sniffing out their hiding places and flaming everything in his path. His rage knew no bounds.

But rage blinded him to a very real threat. Thankfully, Tor had grown up evading such attacks and knew well what to do. Lana knew too. She'd faced these same barbarian warriors while in human form and with a sword at her side, but Roland felt the disturbance of wings flapping awkwardly at his side and he knew she'd shifted to dragon form. Roland cursed inwardly. She was all too vulnerable in the larger form until she was more comfortable in her hide.

Lana, stay back.

No, Roland, he's behind you!

Roland twirled on his talons, facing the new threat. He immediately saw the hate-filled face above the sparkling, diamond-tipped arrow, knocked and ready to slice into Lana's heart. It was Salomar himself.

With a bellow, Roland pushed Lana aside as gently as he could under the circumstances, throwing himself between her and danger. The arrow pierced his shoulder, but he barely noticed, stalking forward as the self-proclaimed king of the Northlands knocked another arrow he would never get a chance to fire.

Tor came from the side and snatched Salomar about the torso, gripped in his strong talons. One stuck through Salomar's shoulder as the Northern bully writhed in pain, blood dripping down his side.

I got him, Roland!

Good job, Tor.

Roland ferreted out the remainder of Salomar's ambush squad. Only one remained alive and he surrendered when Roland advanced on him with death in his eyes. A moment later, the twins arrived with a mob of dragons and knights, ready for battle.

Sorry we're late. I see you've got this well in hand. Trey landed with his twin in the small clearing.

Nice of you to join us, he thought to his brothers. Turning his attention to the company of knights, he noted the interested gazes pinned to the somewhat awkward black dragon at his side. *Jures, take Salomar and his friend into custody and pen them up at the Lair. I'll have questions to ask them both later.*

Aye, my liege.

"Looks like you have some questions to answer as well, sire." Hal rolled his curious eyes over to Lana. "Bless my soul, is that...? Praise the Mother, I never thought I'd ever see a female black dragon."

Well now you have, Lana fumed, nearly tripping over her tail as she craned her neck to look closely at Roland's wounds, *and I suggest you get over it.*

Roland barked a smoky peal of laughter and spread one wing over his smaller mate while the knights stared in wonder. Jures signaled two of the other knights who took custody of the prisoners and tied them securely before slinging them over the backs of their dragons.

Lana, my love, go easy on them. They've been laying bets for weeks on the identity of that third black dragon. I'd say none ever imagined it could be you.

Oh, there was one, sire, Rue put in with a smoky chuckle, *and he has just become a very rich man indeed.*

We need to get back to the Lair so I can treat your wounds. Lana's voice was edged with worry and he cuddled her under his wing to reassure her. They spoke privately, just between their minds on an intimate pathway that was theirs alone.

Don't worry, the arrows didn't hit anything important. It just hurts a bit. But you're right. We need to get to the Lair. Are you well enough to fly or do you want to change back first?

Tor's hurt too. I'll fly, but you'd better tell them not to laugh at my landing if I tumble ass over tea kettle.

Chapter Twelve

As it turned out, Lana made a decent, if not absolutely perfect landing. Roland breathed a sigh of relief since he knew how important it was to her to make a good impression on the knights and dragons alike. He knew they'd love her no matter how she flew or landed. She was the first female black dragon in centuries, the first to bring a wild northern Ice Dragon to their number, the female with a warm, open heart who had mothered the orphaned dragonet and claimed their king's heart. For all those reasons, they would love her, as well as for her kind, brave soul.

He knew the dragons would chuckle good-naturedly as she learned to fly—she was, after all, the oldest fledgling they'd ever seen—but she was sensitive and he didn't want her to feel badly this first time out in public. The moment she landed, she scrambled behind Tor and shifted back to human form. He knew she hid because thinking her clothes back onto her body was still somewhat problematic, but he was relieved to see this time, the clothing came back with her as she stepped out to tend to their wounds. A worried frown marred her lovely features and he couldn't wait to shift so he could kiss it away.

Studiously ignoring the knights and dragons gathered 'round to watch, he felt her lay her hot little hands on his wounds and pulse healing power into the shallow cuts. They healed quickly with her attentions.

176

Thank you, my love. Go help our boy. He's being very brave, but I know the arrow that grazed his foreleg must've stung like a hornet.

Roland walked over to the dragonet, changing as he moved, so he could catch Lana about the waist with one strong arm and stroke Tor's long neck with the other as the youngster shivered with a bit of pain. Of the two, Roland had gotten the more serious wound so he understood why Lana had tended him first, but he knew she was torn seeing the two males she loved most in the world both hurt and needing her help.

"It's all right, sweetheart, Lana's here," she crooned. "You were very brave." She placed her hands over the baby dragon's foreleg and healed him with just a slight jolt of her expanding power.

"Stars above, she's a powerful dragon healer." Collin's whispered words were loud in the pronounced silence of the Lair's landing ledge. A crowd had gathered to watch, including Roland's twin brothers, now changed into human form.

"And a sister of the skies, as well," Trey confirmed with pride in his voice, speaking loudly so all could hear his amazing words.

Roland knew Lana's little secret was well and truly out now. The dragons would spread word of a female black dragon far and wide among their kind, and the knights would talk about her among themselves and with their dragon partners. He hugged her close to his side as they straightened and faced the assembled knights and dragons.

"As most of you saw, Lana recently discovered she can fly." A great cheer went up from knights and dragons alike at his pronouncement, and he felt Lana tremble at his side, but one look at her flushed face told him it wasn't in fear. She was game, and he was damned proud of her.

When they quieted down a bit, he continued. "We haven't announced it officially yet, though we've told most of my brothers. I'd like you, the knights and dragons of the Northern Lair—the place I spent a good deal of my youth—to know first. Lana has consented to be my wife."

The cheering doubled, joined by the dragons' triumphant trumpeting. It seemed everyone came out to the open area of the landing ledge to wish them well and Roland included Tor in the circle of love, encircling his silvery neck with one arm, clearly claiming the baby dragon for all to see.

"As soon as we can arrange a formal ceremony, Draconia will once again have a queen," Roland said as his brothers came to stand beside them.

"And this queen, unlike any in centuries," Collin said to the crowd, "will rule the skies along with the land."

The cheering renewed and intensified, if that were possible. Roland knew these good people needed a reason to celebrate after the stress and losses they'd suffered in the recent battles. He and Lana enjoyed the congratulations of the gathered knights for a while longer, but it had been a long day, even though it was still only mid-afternoon, and Roland wanted some time alone with his wife-to-be. It had been too long since they made love. Too long since they'd affirmed the life they'd almost lost that morning.

Roland guided her through the crowd, asking Rue and Tilden silently to look after Tor for a bit. The youngster was already seeking out his little friend Rena for playtime, and Roland figured the dragon deserved a bit of frolic and fun after the rough time they'd all had that morning. Roland felt like frolicking with a certain pretty girl himself— but in a much more adult way.

"Ready for some alone time?" His words were for Lana's ears only as they moved through the dispersing crowd.

She looked up at him with sparkling, mischievous eyes. "I'm always ready for you, Roland."

"Are you now?" He looped one arm around her shoulders as they walked. Off to their left, he watched Tor and little Rena take off from the ledge, followed closely by Tilden and Rue "Seems to me, you told me something like that once before."

"Glad you were listening," she murmured, her small body fitting perfectly into his side as they walked down the wide hall toward their suite.

"Too bad we're not at the castle," he mused as they turned a corner, closer now to their chambers. "I'd show you my dungeon."

Her brows scrunched together in delightful confusion. "Your brother said something about that once before, but why in the world would I want to see a place like that? Salomar's dungeons were icy, cold, barbaric places."

"Ah," he squeezed her shoulders comfortingly, "you're thinking of an altogether different kind of dungeon. We don't have torture chambers in my land—at least not the kind of torture you're thinking about."

"What other kind of torture is there?"

He smiled down at her as he pushed the big door to their suite open wide and ushered her inside. "The best kind of torture there is— sensual, sexual torture, my dear." She gasped as she moved past him into the suite and he closed the massive door. Turning, he caught her around the waist and pushed her up against the nearest wall, tucking his knee right up between her legs. "My dungeon is a place of pleasure, where I will tie you up and make love to you for long, long hours, keeping your senses on the brink of ecstasy. You'll love every minute of it. I promise."

"I—" She stuttered a bit, her lovely green eyes wide with excitement and the unknown. "I don't know what to say, Roland. I had no idea such things existed."

He leaned down and kissed her gently, hoping to still her fears while keeping her eagerness for his touch high. He pulled back, glad to see the tiny wrinkle of anxiety recede from her expression.

"They do indeed exist, and I'll teach you all about them. In time. You need never fear anything we will do together, Lana, or anything I might ask of you. I will push your boundaries, but never exceed them. I vow it." He held her gaze with serious intent. "I will never hurt you."

All tension left her expression as she smiled softly. "I know that, Roland." She reached up and kissed him. "I love you," she whispered against his lips.

He would never grow tired of hearing those words from this special woman—the one who would be his wife, and his queen. He knew his land and people could do no better than to have Lana as their mistress and he could have no better partner in passion than she. He needed her again, even now. It seemed he was in a perpetual state of readiness whenever she was around. Hell, his cock got hard when he simply thought of her, never mind when she was near.

Moving decisively, he backed away from the wall, swung her into his arms, and strode for the bedchamber. He needed a bit of privacy for what he intended. It was time to start pushing her boundaries just a bit.

Lana was thrilled by Roland's display of power. After seeing him hurt and healing his injuries, she'd run a full gamut of emotions—

terror, agony and then blessed relief when she knew he would be all right. The events of the morning had brought home to her just how precious he was, and how much a part of her heart he held already. She'd been ready to die for him, but he'd jumped in front of an arrow meant for her.

She would never find a braver, more honorable, or sexier mate than the one the Mother of All had brought her in Roland. He was her other half. He completed her, and she suspected—no, she knew—he felt the same. She had confidence in his declaration of love. He'd proven himself time and again, and she trusted him with her body, and her heart.

He shouldered open the door to the bedchamber and kicked it shut forcefully behind them. With no warning, he bounced her onto the wide bed, following her down onto it almost immediately. He spared no time for niceties, the fire in his emerald eyes brighter than she'd ever seen it. Roland seemed almost out of control as he ripped at his shirt, literally scattering buttons in all directions.

Lana tried to sit up, but he pushed her back down and straddled her hips. He moved up her torso, kneeling step by kneeling step, until his leather-clad crotch rested somewhere between her breasts and her chin.

"Undo the knot in my leggings, Lana." His eyes smoldered as he looked down at her.

She moved awkwardly to bring her hands up around his muscular thighs, but he caught her wrists and held them at his hips. With deft fingers, he spread her palms until they cupped his ass.

"Don't move your hands," he chastised. "Now, undo the knot, Lana," he paused slightly, "With your teeth."

Her breath caught on a gasp as she read the challenge in his gaze. Apparently this was a bit of that boundary-expanding he'd been talking about just a minute ago, and damned if she wasn't excited by the forceful way he pushed her to new experiences. She already felt the slippery slide of excitement between her legs.

Lana leaned up, stretching her neck to reach the tie that held his leggings together. She knew well he was bare beneath and could see the outline of his hard cock under the supple leather even now. Lana licked her lips in anticipation and tried to do as he commanded. It wasn't easy, but after a few fumbles, which she knew he enjoyed by the gasps and growls issuing from his throat, she managed to tug the knot free and work the lacings loose until his cock sprang out. Roland wasted no time, moving forward so that his hard cock was directly in front of her mouth.

"Open, Lana. Take me in your mouth."

She read the excitement in his eyes as her own passion burned hotter. She loved pleasing this man, no matter what he asked. She opened her mouth and sucked him down deep, loving the way he filled her. His aggressiveness nearly overwhelmed her at first—but in the most exhilarating way.

"That's it, love. Tongue me. Lick me up and down. All over." His breathing came in harsh pants as his balls tightened. He began to thrust lightly, all the way to the back of her throat. "Suck it now, love. Suck it hard!"

He increased his motion as she followed his orders, and when he exploded, she struggled to keep up. Roland saw her distress and immediately backed off. He climbed off her and rolled to his side on the large bed. Watching her, he caressed her cheek with one big hand and caught a spilled drop of his liquid. With his thumb, he stroked his essence into her skin

"I love you more than life, Lana. There's so much I want to show you."

Lana's body still hummed with eagerness, but Roland was done. What now? she wondered.

Roland wasn't done with her. Not by a long shot.

The beast within sated for the moment, he could now devote himself to his lady's pleasure in devious and delicious ways. He had plans for Lana. Plans that included giving her as much pleasure as she'd just given him…and more. As much as he could possibly give.

His strength returning after a mind-bending orgasm, Roland shifted to his knees at her side. He grasped the edges of her dress in his hands, near the collar, and tore the garment down the middle in one swift move. Lana shrieked and he liked the sound. It was surprise, not fear, and he vowed to surprise her again and again as her taught her the kinds of games he knew she would enjoy.

Roland continued ripping the fabric until she was bare beneath him and threw the shreds of fabric away over his shoulder, never taking his attention away from the female flesh before him. He did keep a few little peices of the soft cloth nearby, though, for later use. When she was naked, he pushed her legs apart forcefully, liking her gasp as he manhandled her just a bit.

"Do you like that, my sweet? Do you like it when I touch you with a little edge of roughness?"

Wide-eyed, she nodded.

"You must answer aloud when I ask a question, sweetheart. Say, 'yes, my liege,' or 'no, my liege.' Do you understand?"

She hesitated only a moment as he spread her arms wide above her head. "Yes, my liege." Her voice trembled, but he knew it wasn't in fear.

Deliberately, he picked up one of the shreds from her dress and looped it around her wrist. Her luminous eyes grew even wider and he had to suppress a chuckle.

"I'm going to tie you up, Lana. I want you at my complete mercy. Is that all right?" He had to ask. He had to have her with him in this game. It was imperative to bring her with him every step of the way, lest some fear or misunderstanding mar this experience.

At length, she nodded and he tweaked one rosy nipple. "Remember what I said about answering. Aloud, Lana."

She was quicker this time. "Yes, my liege." Her tone was breathless with eager anticipation.

He set to work, drawing out the steps of tying first her right wrist to the bedpost, and then her left. She watched his every move and her breathing increased as her excitement grew. When he was done with her wrists, he climbed between her spread legs and looked at his handiwork.

She was wet. Glistening with excitement. Her little bud was quivering with need already. Oh, she really did like this game, as he'd suspected she would. After all, she was perfect for him in every other way.

He ran one finger down her slick folds, pausing to rub around her clit, and her hips nearly bucked off the bed. He held her down and felt the flow of her desire increase a bit.

But it wasn't yet time.

Leaning to his side, he ran his hand from pussy to ankle, slowly and seductively. He liked the gooseflesh that rose on her thighs as he stroked her. She was with him, thrilling to his touch.

With sure, deft movements, he secured her ankle to the lower bedpost, leaving a little leeway so she could bend her knees a bit. He then tied the other ankle the same way, sitting back on his haunches between her widely spread legs when he was done, with a deep sense of satisfaction. She was beautiful. And so responsive.

"You're mine." Roland's voice was a deep growl he almost didn't recognize as the dragon in him roared inside his mind. "You understand that, don't you?"

"Yes, my liege."

He could have crowed at her quick affirmative. Instead, he moved swiftly, depositing playful, snarling, biting kisses over her slightly rounded tummy and hips. As he shifted lower, his playful nips turned to licking sweeps of his tongue and teasing scrapes of his teeth over her soft thighs. She had the finest skin he had ever beheld, creamy and pure, and the soft texture of silk. He moved lower and settled between her thighs, pressing them wider with the span of his shoulders as she moaned.

"Let me hear your cries, sweetheart. Let me hear your passion." His words whispered against her inner thigh, but he knew she heard him from the increase of her sobs as he parted her slick folds and stroked his tongue within. She tasted like the sweetest ambrosia, delicious and addicting to the dragon that lived within him.

"That's it," he growled against her, "let me know what you're feeling." He redoubled his efforts, sweeping his tongue around and over the little nubbin, and almost had her crying out.

But not yet.

He pulled back slightly and raised his head to meet her eyes.

"Now I'm going to kiss you," he stated, loving the confusion that flickered in her eyes. "Do you want my kiss, Lana?"

"Oh, yes, my liege." Her breathy whisper nearly made him break into a smile, but he held firm. How he loved teasing his woman.

"Would you beg for my kiss, Lana?"

She nodded, holding his gaze. "Yes, my liege. I'm begging you now. Please kiss me."

"Where do you want me to kiss you, Lana?" He liked the look of desperate yearning on her face, and the shocked puzzlement that crossed her lovely features a moment later as she digested his words.

"Anywhere! Anywhere you want, my liege." She writhed as her excitement rose higher yet. She evidently liked his teasing talk.

"Coward," he scolded softly, cajoling. "Tell me where you want me to kiss you, Lana. Come on, be the daring woman I know you to be. Beg me to kiss your pussy, Lana. You know you want to."

"Oh, stars! Roland, I'm begging you!"

"What?" he pulled back, reminding her of his role in this game.

"My liege! My liege. I'm begging you, my liege." Her head rolled side to side, just a bit, as desperation nearly consumed her. She was so close. But he would push her still further.

"What *exactly* are you begging for, Lana?" His quiet words purred through the bedroom.

"I'm begging for your mouth, my liege. Your mouth on my pussy. Please! Please, Roland. My liege!"

Oh, he liked that. Roland took his time, stretching the moment out.

"That was nicely done, Lana. And now, your reward." He moved slowly, noting the increase in her little shivers. Lowering his head, he spread her outer lips and settled his mouth over her, stroking his tongue deep within, kissing her as she'd begged him to do. With one thumb, he stroked the little nub as her cries shook the rafters of the room, her climax exploding in a great thundering rush.

Roland rode her throughout, extending the pleasure, until she began to settle back down. He then rose swiftly to his knees and ripped the tattered fabric that held her ankles to the bedposts, freeing her legs with his dragon's strength. Pushing his unlaced leggings down and out of the way, he pulled her bare legs up around his waist and sank into her warmth with all possible speed.

Oh, how he needed this! He needed her warmth, her surrender, her love. And he had it all. He knew that without a doubt. He had her, as she had him, and they would never part.

He'd thought, for one desperate moment that morning, that she would die. His entire life had flashed before him. In that moment, he knew he'd die gladly to protect this woman. His woman. And without her, he would never be whole again. Without her, he didn't want to live.

But she was here, beneath him, a piece of him now, and nothing would part them. Ever. Roland stroked deep within her hot depths, loving her impassioned cries, capturing them on his tongue as he kissed her mouth, plunging his cock deep within his woman. His lover. His love.

Lana's legs wrapped around his waist, squeezing his flanks as she urged him faster, and he obeyed. Roland's pace increased and soon they shot to the stars once more. Together.

As they would be now…for always.

CRCRCR

Sometime later, Roland and his brothers questioned Salomar and the soldier caught with him at length, learning a great deal about conspiracies that all seemed to trace back to Skithdron and its mad king. Salomar was little better than King Lucan of Skithdron and the two had formed an unholy alliance to try to overtake Draconia.

One startling fact they learned from Salomar was that Lucan had sent team after team of explorers into the far north looking for...something. Salomar didn't seem to know all the particulars, but he confessed Lucan was after some rare, ancient artifact of magic and was willing to equip Salomar's army with the costliest diamond blades in order to attain safe passage through the Northlands for his search parties.

Roland planned to transport Salomar and his minion to the castle for further interrogation and imprisonment, but even as the knights did their best to subdue him, Salomar broke his bonds and made a run for it. Unfortunately he took a tumble and sailed over the edge of the Lair's landing ledge before anyone could get a hand on him, crashing to his death on the rocks far below. A few scouts were dispatched to retrieve the body and bury it properly, for Roland believed even his worst enemy deserved a proper burial. After Salomar's soldier saw his leader die, he was surprisingly eager to tell what little he knew and went with the guards with little fanfare.

The Northern Lair held a huge banquet to celebrate their victory, as well as to welcome their new sister of the skies and future queen. Prince Nico even arrived just in time for the party, much to his brothers' surprise and amusement. Nothing, it truly appeared, was hidden from the Prince of Spies.

It was the first of many feasts Roland and Lana would attend at the various Lairs and, of course, back at Roland's castle, but this one was special. As she thought back on it later, Lana realized this celebration marked the wedding of their hearts, though a state wedding with all the pomp and circumstance would be held at the castle later.

No, it was the people and dragons who made this celebration stand out. That, and the fact that after the dancing and feasting, Lana and Roland made their first mating flight, much to the delight of the dragons and knights alike. The two black dragons soared to the stars together, other dragon pairs all around them in the twinkling night sky, joining them in ecstasy as they flew and fell with their life mates. It was the first time in centuries two black dragons had made the flight, and it marked the beginning of a new era for the dragons and knights alike. They trumpeted their joy as they joined their king and queen in happiness and pleasure.

A new day was dawning in Draconia, and though there were still enemies on the horizon, for the moment, at least, there was peace, joy, and most important of all...love.

Epilogue

Under cover of darkness, the black dragon slipped across the border into Skithdron, his black hide blending with the night. Nico truly was the Prince of Spies and he was on a noble quest. The North Witch Loralie had told Lana her sister was in Skithdron, but Nico's agents had been even more specific.

Aside from the girl, Nico had some spying to do on the Skithdronian king and his troops. Things were not yet settled between the two kingdoms, and though they had so far held back, Nico knew more violence was coming. Such was the way with tyrants.

Roland had taken care of the tyrant to the north and now celebrated with his new queen. It would be up to Nico to gather enough intelligence to defeat the tyrant to the east.

Mission firmly in mind, Prince Nico landed on the outskirts of the capital city hours later, changing swiftly and secretly from dragon to human form. His contact would meet him shortly, hopefully with the information he needed—or at least another piece to the puzzle that was slowly taking shape.

Nico was eager, but not stupid. He'd checked over the area from above while still cloaked in the darkness of his dragon shape. The immediate area of the pre-arranged meet seemed clear, but Nico approached cautiously, eyes wary for any sign of trouble.

When it came though, trouble still caught him by surprise. A troop of royal guards had him surrounded before he could react. He dared not change to dragon form in front of so many witnesses. Odds were he couldn't kill them all before escaping, and the secret of the royal blacks was too precious to reveal so clumsily. He would hold that in reserve.

For now, Nico allowed himself to be shackled and led away toward the palace. He wanted to get a look inside King Lucan's palace anyway, though he would have chosen another method had it been left up to him. Still, this would get him in. Once inside, he had little doubt he would be able to free himself. There wasn't a chain or shackle made that could hold a black dragon.

With an eager stride, Nico went to face whatever waited. There was more at stake in this game than just his own safety. No, Draconia itself was at stake here, and the safety of his land and people was more important than anything.

About the Author

A life-long martial arts enthusiast, Bianca enjoys a number of hobbies and interests that keep her busy and entertained, such as playing the guitar, shopping, painting, shopping, skiing, shopping, road trips, and did we say…um…shopping? A bargain hunter through and through, Bianca loves the thrill of the hunt for that excellent price on quality items, though she's hardly a fashionista. She likes nothing better than curling up by the fire with a good book, or better yet, by the computer, *writing* a good book.

Bianca loves to hear from readers and can be reached through her Yahoo group at through the various links on her website.

Web URL
http://biancadarc.com

Email Addy
Bianca@biancadarc.com

Yahoo Group Link
http://groups.yahoo.com/group/BiancaDArc/join

Look for these titles

Now Available

Maiden Flight: Dragon Knights Book 1
Border Lair: Dragon Knights Book 2
Lords of the Were

Coming Soon:

Forever Valentine
Prince of Spies: Dragon Knights Book 4
Hara's Legacy: Resonance Mates Book 1

First in the Dragon Knights series.

Maiden Flight
© *2006 Bianca D'Arc*

War is coming for the knights, dragons, and a damsel who is not quite in distress, but finds her heart's desire in the strong men of the Border Lair.

A chance meeting with a young male dragon seals the fate of one adventurous female poacher. The dragon's partner, a ruggedly handsome knight named Gareth, takes one look at the shapely woman and decides to do a little *poaching* of his own.

Sir Gareth not only seduces her, but falls deeply in love with the girl who is not only unafraid of dragons but also possesses the rare gift to hear their silent speech. He wants her for his mate, but mating with a knight is no simple thing. To accept a knight, a woman must also accept the dragon, the dragon's mate… and her knight too.

She is at first shocked, then enticed by the lusty life in the Lair. War is in the making and only the knights and dragons have a chance at ending it before it destroys their land and their lives. But there's nothing a knight enjoys more than a noble quest and winning the heart and trust of a maiden is the noblest quest of all.

Warning, this title contains explicit sex and ménage a trois.

Available now in ebook from Samhain Publishing.

Second book in the Dragon Knights series.

Border Lair
© 2006 Bianca D'Arc

War has come to the Border Lair, but as enemies become allies-- and lovers, hope springs anew for the dragons and their knights.

A young widow, Adora raised her daughter by herself, but her girl is married now. Can Adora find a love of her own in the crowded Border Lair? Dare she even try?

Lord Darian Vordekrais is about to turn traitor, giving up his title, his lands, and his home in order to warn the dragons and knights of his treacherous king's evil plan. Will his life be forfeit or is there some way he can make a new life in a foreign land?

Sir Jared lost his wife and child to treachery, but he knows Lord Darian and trusts him. Both men admire the lovely Adora, but Jared's broken heart is frozen in solid ice. Or is it?

As war comes to the border, the knights and dragons of the Border Lair rise to the occasion. New allies rally to their side. Love blossoms and grows even as evil invades the land. The knights and dragons must stand fast against the onslaught, the beautiful woman of royal blood bringing them hope, healing and love.

Warning, this title contains explicit sex and ménage a trois.

Available now in ebook from Samhain Publishing.

How does a lonely tree sprite want to find her man?
Flaming hot!

Tree Sprite
© 2006 Brenda Bryce

First of the Wizard Kin series.

Daniel has left his destroyed mountain home and is in search of a new place to live. He comes across a pretty glade with a single short, round tree occupying it and takes his rest underneath.

Oleafia is a tree sprite, shunned by the surrounding forest sprites, and finding a sleeping man, proceeds to fall out of her tree and onto him. Literally.

Both lonely, they are each what the other needs in their lives. Though the fairy tale world they live in is a harsh one, and they are separate species, it matters little to them. What matters is that they complete each other.

Daniel enthusiastically teaches the lovely, full-figured sprite all about sex and love, and Oleafia is a more than willing student from the moment she sees his huge branch.

Through opposition from other sprites and a spelled glade, will they be able to form an unbreakable bond? Or will they continue on their lonely ways?

Available now in ebook and print from Samhain Publishing.

Enjoy the following excerpt from Tree Sprite...

Within the tree, Oleafia opened her eyes. Something was different. Something had changed. Some*one* had entered her glade. Hmm, this could be interesting.

Oleafia had very few interesting things enter her glade. This, though, could be an opportunity. One she wouldn't miss.

She exited her tree on a central branch and looked around the glade. Sighing, she saw nothing had changed. All the other tree sprites were still shunning her. Nothing would ever change. On the verge of tears, she turned to reenter her tree, when she glanced down. Oh, Goddess. There was a human under her tree.

What is he doing? At least, I think it is a he. The being had curled into a ball and she couldn't see the *important* parts that would enable her to tell what type of human it was. Curious, she crept closer. Closer. She was directly above him.

SNORE.

"*Augh!*" At the startling sound Oleafia lost her hold on the branch and landed on the creature.

"*Oof.*" The grunt erupted from the being.

As she tried to scramble off him, he wrapped his arms around her, holding her immobile. Trapped. Caught. It was definitely a he, she had seen his man-root as she dropped. However, *that* didn't matter anymore. He had total control of her. She couldn't...

"Well now, what do we have here?" His smoky voice caused her to shiver as the heat of his breath whispered against her neck.

"Please do not fell me, human." She snuffled and lay very still.

"Fell?"

"Yes, cut me down. End my life. Expire me. Please don't. I have done nothing to you. Oh, and I won't. I swear. I mean you no harm."

"I don't plan on killing you, girl."

"You don't?"

He sighed. "No, I don't."

She turned in his arms, facing him. "Honest?"

His eyes widened as he stared at her. "You're a sprite."

Oleafia dropped her gaze. "Yes, a tree sprite."

"I can tell. You're as beautiful as I have heard tree sprites to be." He ran his hands over her back, making each bump and ridge tingle and ripple in pleasure. "And softer than I'd expected."

"I'm not beautiful. That's why my tree is here and not with the others. I'm short and round, instead of tall and svelte. I am exiled." With her long fingernail, she harried one of the two matching bumps on his chest. Interesting. It hardened under her ministrations. Surprisingly, her own chest started to tingle.

He interrupted her chest fascination with a question. "What's your name?" He spoke in a gruff whisper.

"Oleafia. What's yours?" She noticed his leaf-green eyes. *Oh, they are very pretty.*

"My name is Daniel." He didn't take his eyes off her. "If you keep doing that I'm going to make love to you, little tree sprite."

Her entire body jerked in shock. "Make love? To me?"

"Absolutely to you. Didn't you hear me when I said you're beautiful?"

Looking at him through narrowed eyes, she placed her hands on his chest and pushed herself upright, legs spread, straddling his body. "I'm not beautiful. Ask anyone."

He groaned low in his chest, which she felt vibrate against her nest. The sensation caused her to squirm until she felt something poking her backside.

"You are very close, Oleafia, to becoming my lover."

Her eyes widened, her curiosity aroused. "Really? You wish me to be your lover?"

"My hard-on doesn't lie, and it wants you sincerely."

"Hard-on? Show me." She inspected him all over, wiggling and turning to see everything she could, but saw nothing resembling a *hard-on*. She did see dark hair so black it was nearly blue, the strong, granite-like features of his face, the hard muscles of his body. He was much more muscular than any male tree sprite she had seen, but not as muscular as the troll she'd glimpsed once or twice, who lived on the other side of the forest. She thought this male was just right. And his skin was smooth. Smooth as a new leaf. Over and over she ran her hands across his chest, enjoying the feeling. But nowhere did she see a hard-on. "Show me, please."

Grinning, he lifted her without strain, turned her, and faced her in the opposite direction, returning her to the straddling position over his body.

Her smile widened. "Oh. So, *that's* a hard-on." She peered over her shoulder at his face. "Can I touch it? Please?"